Lost Girl

Copyright © 2016 by Billy McLaughlin
All rights reserved. No part of this work covered by the copyright hereon may be reproduced or used in any form or by any means – graphic, electronic, or mechanical, including photocopying, recording, taping, or information storage and retrieval systems – without permission of the publisher.

For my cover girl "Nelly"

And all the family and friends who have encouraged me to finally do this x

1.
His eyes flickered just above the dashboard.

The air was thick with persistent smog as the woman lumbered across the cobbles in six-inch heels. She felt a chilling wind bite at her skin until she was so cold that it hurt to even move. In the distance, sparring voices hid behind the cry of the dropping breeze. Her lashes felt heavy as the salt of her tears stung her cheeks and she lamented over the life that she had left behind. Her hair clung to her face, wet and oily, and she fought the urge to twist it round her frigid hands and tear it out. As she headed for the other side of the street, she wanted to climb into the cracks between the cobblestones, and simply disappear. To sleep, undetected, under a spray of iridescent stars.

The car prowled at less than five miles per hour, the lights dimmed so that they were barely visible

Through the barricades of a vodka infused stupor, Kate tried to recall where her life had begun to crumble. She could mentally trace the moment where she had told her husband that she was leaving. She could almost touch the relief she had felt as she took a single bag and crawled out of the ruins of her broken life. What hadn't been so easy, though, was the painstaking search for a life that didn't yet exist. Instead, she had walked away from her house; *her deflated husband in the doorway, her tear-stained child in the window frame*, and found that the world was bitter cold and had virtually nothing to offer her.

He watched as she struggled to stay on her feet, her heels buckling under the weight of her hefty troubles.

The sun had already set at the edge of the world whilst the icy winds blew through the torpors of her mind. Clarity rumbled, but didn't quite materialise. She moved through the lingering haze, drifting and recoiled in defeat, tightening the leather jacket around her breasts. Once upon a time, her life had been so unimaginably bad that she couldn't contemplate staying in it. Now she thought of those days with the nostalgia and tenderness that could only be afforded to fading memories. She could go back, but what little pride she still gripped on to prevented her from pleading with him for another chance. To tell him that the life he had given her hadn't been the worst was too humiliating for her to even consider. Instead, she carried on through the rotting city in search of somewhere to sleep. A box! A house! Anywhere!

She may not have been aware of the presence at first, because she moved slowly and carelessly, swirling inside her selfish thoughts. Even when she glanced at the car in the first instance, it hadn't initially occurred to her that it could be following her. When it did become apparent that the car was moving at the same speed as her, she turned and glowered. It was merely a shadow in the smog, but when she stopped and stared, the car skidded quietly to a halt and froze. At first, she scolded herself for being fearful, but as she quickened her pace, she became aware that the car continued to imitate her speed. The street was relatively empty although the muffled voices became clearer to her as she reached a corner. She wanted to fall into the crowd, to find herself surrounded by normality. To savour the joy of interaction with people who were decent and kind. She had suffered enough embarrassment tonight. So, she allowed the crowd to pass through her with the boundless energy that she could no longer muster. She smacked her tongue against the roof of her mouth and felt the bitter tingle of the vodka she had helped herself to. The crowd had passed now, and she found their joviality almost as jarring as her own loneliness. The car engine snarled, cruising at a pace that was unnervingly slow, prowling behind two strips of ambiguous light. She looked directly at the bonnet and searched for a face. She could see nothing more than a shadow, so she simply walked a little faster.

The river swished in fervour as she slipped round the corner of Clyde Street. She could see the blue ledge of lights from the bridge illuminate the tiny waves below her. Then, as she looked back, she saw the car turn in her direction. Terror grew in the pit of her bowels, twisting upon her stomach until the pain was almost tangible. The car was so close, she could smell the fumes from its exhaust; foul and nauseating. She still couldn't see inside because, other than its dimmed headlights, the car was in complete darkness. Malice rattled from the engine of the car, filling the quiet air with a monstrous savagery. The eyes of intimidation peeked at her as the wheels stopped and started in sync with her. She walked faster than she thought she could even though her ankles ached. The car sped up slightly, but never leaving her side. Who the hell was behind the wheel? She wanted to march back to the roadside, throw a brick through the window, and holler some choice words through the broken glass. What did they want with her?

The city centre of Glasgow was a grid of long flat tarmac that had been designed for traffic to go one way. Had she been a little more lucid, she might have turned in a different direction, putting an appropriate amount of distance between herself and the driver. She stared glumly at the rising river and felt the sudden urge to cry. Even over the swoon of the water, she could hear her heels thud at the pavement, now a flat strip of asphalt. She could jump into the Clyde and be carried into the tide. Who would miss her? Who would even know? Only whoever was slumped behind the wheel of that car. For a second she genuinely contemplated it. A world without Kate Mulgrew. She thought of the pain she had already caused her family and wondered if this would really be any worse. Adrenalin paddled through her every vein whilst terror of the unknown sat unmercifully on her skin. Then, without warning, she threw herself down a grassy incline at the side of the river. She could almost feel the sharp edges of the grass whip at her flesh. She saw the world; its lights and its towering buildings spin so fast that it all blurred to her. Eventually, she stopped at the foot of the grass and felt her elbow slump against the tarmac of the footpath. She was inches from the river's edge now.

Kate didn't move. She lay there for minutes that felt like hours and listened so intently that she thought she might hear a bug move in the depths of the dirt. She daren't even turn her head for fear that the driver of the car would find her at any moment. The roar of its engine had intimidated her when she could see it. Now that she couldn't, she longed to hear it rev its engine and rumble into the distance. Instead, it remained silent and perfectly still. She could almost feel her breath as it fell upon her face. There were no words to describe her fear as it was so all-consuming. She looked up at the constellation of stars as they blanketed the world, but she was too frightened to enjoy the view. The rain began to fall then, a dazzling sheet of silver drops that blackened as tiny puddles formed on the ground around her.   Her ears continued to search for an indication that the car had either stopped or moved on. Then, from the corner of her eye, she saw somebody move. Was it a man? She couldn't see properly. The person moved so swiftly, and the rain fell so rapidly that she couldn't fully comprehend what she was seeing. The person blurred as they leaned over her. She was about to let out a piercing scream when the person reached down towards her and placed their hand across her mouth.

2.

Flames crackled up the walls before licking at the edges of the ceiling. The fire had already burned through everything that was flammable in the room and now flared towards the door. Any minute now, the glass would break in the corroding heat and the fire would spread through the building. For now, it was contained to the reception area. As the window panes shattered in its unbridled rage, the cold breeze fanned the inferno and carried it out into the night air. The leather chairs and the wooden desk had already blackened, transformed to charcoal that would eventually smoulder on the floor. The hue of smoke billowed up as the skyline seethed in its wake. Meanwhile, the flames had finally spread into a storeroom that held copious amounts of flammable liquids, ensuring that the entire building would be scorched and reduced to ashes.

The fire consumed everything in its path, destroying all but the bricks and mortar. Flames blasted through the gaping frames and into the chilly air. Ash floated up and sprinkled like the falling flakes of a wet snowy day. As the sun rose the next morning, embers were still glowing in a fiery celebration of the colossal devastation. Firefighters had been fearful of entering the building because of the sheer vast array of accelerants stored on the first floor. As the cold night turned into a frigid morning, onlookers had arrived to catch a snap shot of the obliteration and unrepentant damage. They lined up just near enough to witness the annihilation of a building that had towered on the hill for longer than many of them could recall.

Seven hours had passed since the blaze had begun. Firefighters had fought gamely through crumbling walls and falling beams, taking it in turns as their oxygen tanks had frittered to nothing with alarming regularity. They searched through the three creaking floors, moving carefully around the charred carcass of the once elegant block. Most of its neighbours knew of its reputation; what it had once been and what it had become. Many had been disgusted when its owner, Bruce Anders, had taken the illustrious area and filled it with the type of woman most people wouldn't want to be associated with. There was nothing left for them to be disgusted by. The whispering innuendo and reputation of its patrons lay dead in the ashes. All of its possessions; merely sticks of wood and melded fabrics, had dissolved to nothing.

At 8.15 a.m. Bruce Anders arrived. He was a tall burly man who had reportedly circled in the seedier side of his business. At forty years old, his body was so toned that his numerous tattoos were separated by the grooves in his skin. His mousy hair was shaved down, almost to the wood of his skull, and funnelled into a flick that complimented his bronzed face and grey eyes. He wore a brown sweater and a pair of Levis jeans as he stepped out of his BMW and stared in shock at the shell of his building. Somewhere in the ashes lay a pyramid of his secrets. If he was a weaker man, he might have fell to his knees and howled to God. He saw the firefighters go in, almost in slow motion, then come back out again. He saw the Chief of fire co-ordinate them almost as if they were on a film lot. As he got closer to the building, stepping through the barricade, his mouth and nostrils were filled with the odious scent.

There was an eerie quiet that hung over the men as they continued to try to salvage the houses on either side of Bruce's building. Both had been rocked by the raging firestorm although the internal cosmetics of both houses had been saved by the arrival of firefighters. Bill Walker, who lived on one side of the building with his wife Elena, exchanged a worried glance with Allison Fields. Allison had only just bought the house on the other side of the lap-dancing club a few months before and had been quite dismayed to discover exactly what she was living next too. She tutted and leaned in to whisper to Mrs Petrie, a busy body who had been watching the whole disturbance unfold since the arrival of the first engine. They all stood at a safe distance where somebody brought them a flask of tea and a cheese sandwich. The three of them had been invited into Mrs Petrie's house at the end of the street, but had refrained because they feared that their house might come rocking to the ground and that they wouldn't be here to see it. Bruce nodded his head in sympathy to them, but wasn't shocked when they simply turned away in revulsion.

A few moments later, pandemonium broke out inside the house. Bruce could hear one of the fire fighters shout and wave vigorously from an upstairs window. Even in his fire helmet, two layered wick jacket and breathing mask, he didn't look safe as he tried to capture the attention of his colleagues. They filed into the building, splitting the eerie silence with the sound of hollering voices. Bruce gasped as two fire fighters emerged from the house and pulled the breathing apparatus from their face. The Chief of Fire moved towards them so that they stood just inches from the barricade. Bruce leaned over.

"Hey, this is my business in that building. Can you tell me what's going on?" The fire Chief turned towards him, his interest suddenly heightened by the arrival of this stranger. He gestured for the firefighters to hush.

"If this is your business, then you'll probably be able to shed more light than we will at this point." He moved with self-assurance, his voice measured as he looked insistently at Bruce. He then lifted the barricade tape so that Bruce could step under it and enter the vicinity. When Bruce attempted to move too far forward, he gestured firmly with his hand for Bruce to move no farther.

"I've only just arrived. I can't even believe it. I've no idea what the hell happened here. I heard on the radio that there was a massive fire in the city centre, but they didn't divulge that actual whereabouts. I can't believe this has happened." The Chief of fire, Jim Gray, looked sympathetically at him, emphatically holding his hand towards Bruce's chest to ensure that he wouldn't push past. It wasn't the first time somebody's business had been ravaged by fire. It also wasn't the first time that somebody had pulled a number on the police and fire service. Until they knew what had happened here, judgement had to be reserved and Bruce Anders had to be treated like every other victim of fire damage. As Gray continued to measure Bruce up with a sympathetic smile, they heard one of the other fire fighters heave as he stumbled towards them. He pulled his mask from his face and spluttered from the depths of his chest.

"Chief, you might want to see this. I think we've found a body."

3.
The hours passed by like clouds across an ocean. The old woman hid inside a dirty old sleeping bag, gently snoring, hugging a St Christopher's necklace as if she were nursing a new-born baby. She had gotten the fright of her life when, out minding her own business, she had stumbled upon the girl lying on the grass verge. She had dragged her, somewhat unwillingly at first, to the safety of the hulking bridge. Capsules of rain fell at either entrance, encasing the arch in silver sheets of dropping water. The bridge itself rose over the river, boasting a pungent scent that seemed worse than anything else that Kate could smell, carrying on to the other side of the city. She looked at the old woman, her chest gently rising under the layers of rags designed to keep her warm. Both women made an amusing contrast. The old woman wore a purple wool hat where strands of silver hair poked out of the edges. Her finger nails were as black as coal and had evidently been the cause of the unforgiving clawing of her skin tissue. Kate, on the other hand, hadn't yet been tainted by the ravages of outdoor living. She still bore the afforded luxuries of her former life, even if they would soon be a desecrated memory. Blonde streaks weaved lightly through her darker roots. She wore little make up, which only accentuated her natural beauty. Her hands, now discoloured from the cold, clutched tightly at the hem of her jacket as she held it tightly around her chest. Her skirt, as the old woman had correctly pointed out, was too damn short for a night like this.

The old woman stirred from a surprisingly solid slumber and grunted. She peered through one eye and saw Kate still sitting at the end of her bundle of clothes. She had offered Kate something to keep her warm, but the silly little twit had refused. She obviously hadn't reached her rock bottom yet, because the old woman knew that when you hit the ultimate low, snobbery wasn't something that you could afford yourself. She sat up quickly and dropped an empty bottle to the ground. Kate averted her gaze for as long as she could before she felt the flush spread across her cheeks. It was the first warmth she had felt all night.

"What?" she finally asked, unable to contain the irritation that tethered the aching temper of her body? The old woman shrugged.

"Nothing, love, I never said a word." She fumbled through some of her clothes and let out a sturdy laugh.

"What?" Kate asked again, this time more firmly. Another shrug from the old woman.

"Not a word. I never uttered a mutter," she paused and smacked her lips together. Kate looked at her revolting teeth, buried under a mask of yellow and black rot, and then she shuddered. The old woman continued. "I think you're running from something. I would say that's your business love. As long as you don't intend bringing any trouble to my house." 'My house?' Kate shuddered again. When the woman turned towards her, she saw her skeletal face in the full light of morning, and she had to look away. Nobody should look that gaunt, she thought, and tried to envisage what life the woman had lived that had led her to laying claim on a square meter of rotting ground and then referring to it, proudly, as her house.

"You got a name?" There was softness in her voice now. Kate paused for a moment whilst she contemplated her answer.

"Kate," she finally offered. The woman nodded her head. She didn't believe that was really the girl's name at all, but she simply accepted it as given. The old woman knew the beauty of anonymity only too well when one lived on the streets. Who was she to judge anybody? "What's yours?"

"It's Florence, as in Nightingale, but my friends and cohorts prefer to call me Flo. So that'll do." Kate didn't believe that was really the woman's name either, and might have laughed at how mistrusting they both seemed if the circumstances had been different and she didn't fear that upsetting the old woman would see her shunted back out to wander the streets. As Flo rose from the mass of clothes, Kate recalled her leaning over her and the foul stench of her hand across her face. She had almost wanted to vomit into the river, but had managed to swallow whatever urge lay in her.

Kate was about to speak again when she was startled by the arrival of a strange man by the bridge entrance. He stood there under the spray of winter, smiling almost manically at Flo, who hadn't yet noticed him. When she finally turned and saw him holding out a bag towards her, she clasped her hand to her chest and gasped.

"You gave me a bloody fright, you bugger." She howled with laughter. "Come in, Detective Morris and meet my new friend. This is… Kate did you say?" She snatched the polystyrene bag from his hand and riffled through it as the Detective introduced himself to Kate. The old woman pulled a feast of food from the bag and spun excitedly on her heals.

"So Kate, I haven't seen you before. How long have you been here?" Kate pulled back and allowed a heavy silence to settle. She dropped her face shyly to the ground and hoped that the uncomfortable silence would lie long enough for him to sense her embarrassment and turn away. He didn't. He simply observed her and, for a moment, admiration came to life. Even in the shadow and dim light of a winter day, her eyes sparkled brighter than a twinset of moons, and he wondered how she had come to be here at all.

"Not long. I got sacked from my job after a fight with my boss. I'll be back on my feet soon." She finally spoke in a hardened whisper and Flo had to lean in tightly to hear what she was saying. Detective Morris did his best to conceal his disbelief. It wasn't his place to get involved in the scrapes of the street people, so he simply nodded and then turned his attention back to Flo.

"Well, the temperature's set to drip to minus three tonight, so get yourselves well wrapped up." He looked at Kate's attire and felt genuinely concerned for her. "And stay out of the rain." He walked towards Flo then. "You know anything about the fire up at Charing Cross." Indeed, Flo was the ears on the street, but she had heard nothing about it. Not a thing.

"I honestly haven't Detective. Thanks for the grub though. I'll share it with Marv and Kate here if she fancies staying another few nights." She waved her hand dismissively.

He gave Kate the once over again, sympathy creeping across his face, and he genuinely hoped that she would take Flo's offer. She was obviously new to the streets and nobody knew them better than the old dear.

Once he had left, Flo laughed wildly and emptied the bag of food onto the bed of rags.

"We'll no starve tonight m'lady." She broke into an animated jig, dancing as much as her arthritis would allow her. Kate smiled at her and felt the urge to lift something from the bed. The food wasn't hers though. She didn't want to presume that Flo would share it with her. Even if she had told the Detective she would. "Come on, you, let's be going now." Flo bundled the items and her clothes frantically into her satchel that looked too small to hold that many items.

"What?" Kate looked dumbfounded. "You're throwing me out?" She realised the stupidity of the question when she eyed her surroundings and looked over the fence at the river. She pushed herself to her feet and walked towards Flo.

"Not throwing you out, you silly girl. We need to get out of here. Mr Morris is okay, but if the uniformed grunters come knocking, they'll likely move us on anyway, so best not give them the chance, eh?" Flo tidied up her little patch and then called over to a man who stirred in a nearby corner. "Right, Marv, make sure nobody comes in here to my house and steals my place tonight. I'll bring you back your favourite, a nice slice of Battenberg for your trouble." Marv grunted in agreement as Flo wagged her finger at Kate. "Come on you, we've got work to do." Kate felt trepidation slither through her, but also felt her curiosity spiked by the spritely hag as she shuffled merrily into the daylight.

"W-w-what kind of work?" she stuttered. Flo looked back, impatience smeared across her wiry jaw. She didn't say another word. She simply walked out into the sheets of rain and didn't bother to look back and see if Kate had opted to follow her or not.

4.

Bruce Anders lived on the top floor of a brand new complex that sprawled across the south of the river. Even in the belly of winter, the windows were so large that the sun light was able to burst through and illuminate the lounge. He was cocooned on the seventh floor, in the penthouse, and had a panoramic view of the East End of Glasgow. If he peered over the ledge of his window, he would see the people beneath him move like scattering insects. Far and wide, they dispersed into the distance, no more than tiny specks under the skyline. Birds travelled into view, carried on a crest of wind and headed for the river, squawking in their travels. Bruce stared flatly from the window and watched as a police car arrived.

Detective Inspector Phil Morris entered the flat approximately five hours after the body had been discovered in the embers. He passed through the hall and sneered at how sterile the place was. Magnolia walls had devoured any hint of personality, whilst the spectacle of expensive furniture made it look like a dreary showroom designed to either impress or depress. There was a scent of disinfectant dripping in the air and, if Phil Morris was a more suspicious man, he might have thought Bruce Anders was deliberately concealing something else. In the lounge, a faux fire roared beneath a fifty five inch LED screen, which lay perfectly dark and dormant. Phil was followed by Detective Donna Barclay, a gentle looking woman with a lively smile. It was Morris who proved to be the more intimidating of the two as he sat, without invite, on a creased leather sofa.

"Detective Inspector Morris, and this is Detective Barclay, from Police Scotland. Nice place you got here." Bruce scanned the room and then smirked at his new arrivals. "Anyway, we just want to ask you some questions about the body that was discovered at your premises," he paused as he looked intently at Bruce, "and also establish if there was anybody with a motive to burn your business to the ground." Bruce shook his head slowly. Introductions had been made, pleasantries exchanged and Morris had declined a beverage on both of their behalves.

"You want to know if I had a motive for burning my business down?" DI Morris snorted, a hint of sarcasm barely hidden inside his laughter. Bruce shook his head as Morris quickly pulled a notepad from his suit jacket.

"I'll start by establishing your whereabouts at the time of the fire. Shall we say between the hours of ten and two, perhaps?" Donna stood in the doorway, politely awaiting invite, blankly burying her distaste for Anders. That invite seemed unlikely to come.

"I was in my bar. I left there at, around, 2 a.m."

"And somebody can confirm this?" Bruce nodded his head confidently. Even if he was as guilty as all hell, Phil Morris had no doubt that he would have armed himself with a cast-iron alibi. His kind didn't leave it to chance, and he certainly didn't dirty his own hands. Morris knew it was a dead end. "So, can you give me a picture of what you actually did at..." he looked at his notepad to check the name of the business "... HEELS?" He looked up from his notepad and waited for a response.

"It's a lap dancing club." Barclay and Morris exchanged a look that barely hid their surprise. They hadn't expected a flat out admission. Truthfully, Morris already knew exactly what the club was, but it was clear to them that Anders was a slippery fish. He saw that his answer had given them pause. He smiled slightly, enjoying that he had thrown the gauntlet down and that they now had to run through it.

"A brothel?" It was Donna that spoke now, raising an eyebrow in judgement.

"No! It's exactly what I say it is. It's a lap-dancing club. No side orders. No extras." His lips had thinned slightly, and she made a mental note of how quickly he could go from one temperament to the next without warning. She didn't believe a word of it, but she smiled complacently and allowed the men to carry on baiting each other.

"And you own it alone?" Morris re-composed himself and found a different track of questions. Bruce shrugged.

"I have some investors, a few interested parties, but I'm not at liberty to divulge their names." Morris felt a grain of annoyance. Anders wasn't just a slippery fish, he was a cocky one, and there was nothing Morris liked more than to kick the living shit out of somebody's cockiness.

"I may need those names at some point, Mr Anders. After all, it is a murder investigation I'm conducting, not a Public Relations puff piece." He scribbled something illegible on the notepad and turned back. "Do you know anybody with a grudge against you, your business, or… your silent partners?" Bruce could think of numerous people, but none that he would be willing to divulge to the police. He could, and would, take care of most of them himself. One, in particular, came to mind.

"In the game I'm in Detective, I'm sure you'll appreciate that there is always competition." Morris smirked.

"And do you think the competition would turn to arson to get rid of you?" Morris had grown up in the East End of Glasgow during the ice-cream van wars and had seen many taxi firms burned out of business over the years. It didn't shock him that this kind of practice took place in this type of business.

"So, it was arson?" Bruce swept swiftly onto Morris' last statement. Donna narrowed her eyes and moved into the room slightly.

"We haven't ruled it out yet, but we're still waiting on forensics. Were you having any financial difficulties, Mr Anders?" Bruce's brow furrowed slightly, and Donna was sure she saw a flash of anger as he sucked a pocketful of air in, but it passed so suddenly that she couldn't nail it down.

"Detective, I have three bars, a gym and a lap dancing club. I also have various properties throughout the city that I rent out. Do you think I'm having financial difficulties?" Morris merely shrugged and smacked his lips. Anders was the type of guy he would have smacked out before he had joined the force; a womanising, arrogant, piss pot of a guy who had landed on his feet through a charm offensive and brain for numbers.

"It may be worth pulling your accounts. I'm assuming it would take you a few days to do that? It's something we may be interested in at a later date." He spoke matter-of-factly, peering at Donna from the side of his eye. She had barely moved since they had entered the flat, and her expression had rarely changed.

"I think you'd need a warrant to request those, Detective, and at the moment I don't think you've got grounds for a warrant, have you?" Phil Morris rose angrily from the seat, so that he was now standing eye to eye with Bruce Anders. Even though he didn't get louder, there was a quiet roar creeping into his voice now.

"I have a bloody dead body, Mr Anders. A dead body that died horrifically in a fire that looks to be started deliberately at YOUR property. I don't give a shit if you're in business with the prime minister, or if you're down to your last penny. If I suspect, and at the moment I haven't ruled it out that you are at all involved Mr Anders, I will personally escort you to jail myself. Now, the only other thing I need from you now is a list of those who hold a grudge against you. Don't give me bullshit about competition. A man like you doesn't get to run half the entertainment in Glasgow without cracking a few nuts,," he paused long enough to scratch an itch on the bridge of his nose. He noted the cockiness had gone from Bruce now, and that the man was simply nodding in agreement. "While you're at it, I'll need a list of your employees, particularly at the... lap dancing club. I'll also need a list of your ex-employees. I wouldn't reserve that to your club though. Anybody you've sacked in the past year, from any of your businesses, would count as a grudge." Bruce nodded limply. "I will need you to come down to the station and make an official statement."

Morris enjoyed a fleeting moment of satisfaction as he saw the discomfort swim across Bruce's face. He had already decided that this guy was guilty of something. Maybe he hadn't burned his business to the ground. Maybe he hadn't even hired somebody else to do it. However, he wore guilt like a badge of honour and Morris was determined to prod him until he was singing it from the top of his seventh floor penthouse.

"Now, Mr Anders, I have to get to the bottom of a dead body, so I'll need your co-operation." Bruce nodded his head again, aware that he had said very little but perhaps given too much away. He wasn't sure that he should speak to Morris again without some legal advice. What if this copper decided that he was guilty? He needed to lawyer up; *just in case*. That would be later though once they had finally left. "One other thing, Mr Anders; do you have CCTV that we can access?" Bruce looked pensive for a moment.

"Not for the club. All the CCTV is backed up to a system on the premises. I'm sure that'll have been destroyed. It didn't cover every room anyway so I doubt if it will tell you what you need to know. Now, if you don't mind, I have a meeting in half an hour, but I'll get that list for you ASAP, Detective," he muttered and escorted Donna Barclay and Phil Morris to the door. Donna wasn't sure that Bruce fully appreciated the implication of finding a dead body on his premises, nor did she think he was taking it seriously enough. She saw the wry smile on Morris' face as he revelled in his small victory. She gave Bruce Anders a light wave and moved towards the stairs. He watched them begin their descent down seven flights and then slammed his door so hard that the walls shook. A droplet of sweat lay wedged inside a solitary crease on his forehead. He wiped it away and gasped. Searching through his contacts, he arrived at the person he wanted to contact. After a few seconds, the phone began to ring. Once... twice... three times. The call connected.

"It's me," Bruce paused to catch his breath. "Where the hell are you?" He listened as the voice wavered and then whispered to him. "Okay, well that's not important now." He watched as Morris and Barclay moved towards the marked vehicle outside. "Listen to me carefully. I don't care what you're doing right now or how long it takes. I want you to find that bitch Kate Mulgrew and cut her pretty face from cheek to chin. You got me."

5.

The scent of wood polish filled the room as Peter Dow entered his chamber and moved to the side of his desk. Reaching for the remote of an old record player, he slipped a vinyl on to the turntable. The Celtic instrumentation of an Enya record bellowed from the speakers, crackling quietly beneath the sound of the percussion. He pulled the crumpled sheet of paper from his inner pocket and read quickly through his lines once again. The speech had been written for him and, in actual fact, he barely agreed with half of the policies that he would be discussing. He ran his chubby fingers through a mass of curly hair that had been gelled atop his scalp. The main agenda today was the regeneration of the Glasgow River Clyde. Plans to open two new homeless units in the East End of Glasgow had met with fierce opposition from a small local committee. Despite the demonstration against the units, the plans had been pushed through with the desire of clearing out the Clyde's growing vagrant population.

    He smoothed the crinkles in his suit jacket as he left his office and headed for the steps at the front of the town hall. Standing at the microphone, he was almost blinded by the array of flashing lights. He tussled with his tie, an assertion of authority that he had learned at the beginner school of politicians, and then wiped his perspiring hands on the back side of his trousers. As had been predicted, the majority of the audience were local reporters either already in the press or trying to make their way through blogs that were growing in popularity. There was a ruefully low amount of local constituents in the crowd, an indictment of the growing apathy to the lies of power hungry sociopaths.

    Peter stood at the door of the town hall, his back reflected onto a glass encasement between the supporting beams of the building. He hated these tedious moments. It was difficult for him to serve these people when he privately degraded them for their lack of intelligence and abundance of messy emotions. However, he would enjoy the nice article and the photo opportunity that would follow and further aid his own agenda. Now, he delivered his speech with the conviction and delivery of a theatre actor. He spoke of the upcoming elections, his dedication to pouring endless riches onto the poor people of a dwindling Port, and the need for more transparency within local government. It was a speech worthy of a BAFTA because neither he, nor they, believed a word of it. When he finally stopped speaking, a small middle aged woman lifted her hand to ask a question.

"I want to know what the hell you plan to do about the scum living in my block. I've got three addicts up my close. Last week I thought they were going to stab each other. You should have heard it. Disgusting! We're all sick of it." Peter felt his shoulders sag, and he desperately wanted a drink. Moreover, he wanted to crawl into a nearby drain and disappear. It was the exact reason he hated addressing at local level. They didn't understand the real agendas, or the long scope that he was aiming for. He cleared his throat and smiled awkwardly, rubbing his hand across his stubble.

"Well, naturally Mrs...?"

"Mrs Mackie." She was a dour woman in a grey cardigan and brown corduroy trousers. Her face was framed with massive spectacles that belonged in a different era, and a set of yellow teeth that Peter wasn't sure even belonged to her.

"Mrs Mackie. We do have the neighbourhood office where you can make a complaint about anti-social behaviour. We only know about these things if you bring them to our attention." He deliberately averted his eyes and was about to move onto another raised hand when she heckled his attention back to her.

"Report it. You've got to be kidding. Half the workers in the neighbourhood office are too busy drinking coffee and doing their nails. Mr Dow, you don't know what it's like living down here. We're frightened of being murdered in our beds." There it was! The histrionics had begun, and they were only five minutes into the Question and Answer section of his press conference. Another woman piped up then, much younger and more akin to a biker who ate razor blades for breakfast.

"Yeah, you come and live here Mr Dow. We'll bed up in your flash town house or two hundred k flat in the city centre, and you can shrivel up behind the door, feirt to open it while neds and druggies are full of whatever street crap they're on. Yards from our weans and grand weans." Peter daren't argue with the second woman, so he simply wiped his forehead, dismissing his growing anxiety.

"I have a clinic every Tuesday, if you fine ladies would like to discuss this more; we can talk about it then." He wanted to throttle Mrs Mackie. To take the wire of his microphone and wrap it round her scrawny neck until she didn't have to worry about being murdered in her bed anymore. One less hysterical constituent to contend with. Instead, he simply turned to the reporter who was anxiously waving his hand about now and gave him his opportunity to speak.

When the press conference came to an end, Peter returned to his office and prepared for his five o'clock meeting. He grabbed the late edition of today's Port Times and rested his right leg on the table. Leaning back on his chair, he read the front-page headline and instantly felt his body falter. He saw the room move slightly as if someone were pulling the wall away from him. He held on to the edge of the desk, his suit jacket brushing against the oak ledge. He couldn't focus on anything other than the headline. Even the words below were difficult to put into sentences. He read the headline aloud as if throwing it into the air would help it make sense.

"BODY FOUND IN LAPDANCING FIRE,"

He stood up and felt his mind swirl. He staggered back and reached for the bottle from his cabinet. The bottle met the glass, chinking it in the process, and Peter felt the forty year old malt swim in his mouth and rub against his palate. He thought of his own dalliance at HEELS, and the girl's he had met. Now, he felt sick. Who was she? Was it somebody he himself had encountered? He felt the malt burn at his throat as the bile in his gut formed and rose in his chest. Finally, when he could endure it no more, he leaned over into the plastic waste paper bin and vomited the contents of his lunch.

6.
"So, who are you running away from?" Kate walked a step behind Flo and watched as she scraped her rotting finger nails across the shop windows. Kate didn't answer. She shrugged her shoulders, childlike, as Flo eyed her distrustfully. The old woman still hadn't revealed the nature of this work that they had to do. She had talked incessantly since early noon when they had ventured out from under the bridge. It was evident to Kate that she was no run-of-the-mill homeless woman. Flo had dined in fine restaurants, drank from the chalice of the rich, and slept in beds befitting of Queens. How had she come to consider the litter of cardboard boxes beneath the bridge as her stately home? Each day, she packed up her little sack of belongings, threw them over her corroding back bone, and ventured into the streets. She didn't beg. In Flo's opinion, and she had many of those; begging was a crass act that borrowed on the humility of other people. So, she had dumped her sack at Kate's feet on the corner of Argyll Street, and dragged her offensive stench into Bannister's Bargains.

The aisles were lined with food items and an array of household junk. Flo ran her fingers across the dusty ledges and eyed an assortment of treasure. The shop no longer had the threat of a security guard. Instead, it had opted for a life size window sticker of PC Plod, which could only entice the local homeless community to steal more. She had laughed heartily the first time she had seen that and almost wanted to shake his hand for making it so easy for her. As she wrestled through the bargain hunters, she poured food items into the deceitfully large breast pocket of her coat. If she was concerned that anybody was watching, she certainly didn't show it. In fact, there was nonchalance to her act that suggested either disregard for the law or a bewildering desire to be caught and apprehended.

Kate stood on the corner and watched the traffic come from every junction. The jostle continued as people pushed past other people to get to the traffic lights. There was an urgency that amused Kate as she noted that many were going in the same direction within the same time frame. As she continued to stand, eager to blend into the background, she realised that her unkempt appearance and hefty sack probably had the reverse result.

"Kate?" The voice came from the crowd, and she couldn't quite see who was calling for her. Dread lifted and settled on her shoulders, weighing heavily upon her. She crooked her neck, trying to find the source of the voice. A woman? Was it Flo? No, she sounded too young to be Flo. Besides, whatever mischief the old dear would get herself into would likely take longer than this.

"Kate, it's me, Jennifer." Jennifer practically poured herself into Kate's freezing arms, hugging her too tightly for somebody she had barely known. She recognised the girl, but it was difficult to visualise her in these surroundings. "How are you? I was wondering what had happened to you."

"Oh, hey! Yeah, how are you?" Kate's awkward smile seemed at odds with Jennifer's enthusiastic gait. Jennifer must have sensed her embarrassment because she moved round to stand at her side, carefully sidestepping the hulking sack that Kate had been left to babysit.

"Yeah, I'm good. So what happened to you? Did the bastard sack you? One day you were there and then the next... just gone!" She smiled as if she had found a long-lost friend. It unnerved Kate. "So where are you staying? I've got me a place in the West End. It's lovely, much better than the hostel I was in last week. So you hear about HEELS? Burned to the ground." Heels! Kate had tried not to think about that sordid place, or Bruce Anders, or the variety of girls who she had come into contact with at HEELS. Jennifer was like a freight train. Her words came rushing at Kate at eighty miles per hour, and it made her feel quite faint. Where was Flo? She stared back at the entrance to the shop and sighed heavily.

Flo shuffled to the door of the shop, smiling shamelessly until the onlookers averted their eyes. She daren't smile, though, at the two shop assistants who routinely packed small bags for paying customers. As she approached the door, she decided she would also have a pack of gum. The queue of buyers watched her in equal measure of despair and amusement. Her frowzy appearance aged her enough to convince them that she was a harmless old soul in desperate need of a good wash and a bowl of hot soup. As she stood between the counter and the exit, she purposely knocked a tall stand of key rings and greeting fridge magnets onto the floor. The contents splattered everywhere and created an almighty calamity.

"Right, come on you. OUT!" shrieked the man-boy who had been serving a woman old enough to be Flo's mother, but who looked exactly the same age. As he moved round his colleague to escort her to the door, she grabbed a packet of spearmint gum and pushed it quickly into her pocket. "Don't think I don't know that you have got half a week's worth of shopping in that jacket." He minced past the blow of mayhem she had caused, halting in front of her just far enough to avoid the reek of her odour, and ensured she could see the accusatory look upon his face.

"How bloody dare you, you flaming Jessie," she roared, bellowing her indignation across the entire store. "I'm a fine upstanding woman and have never stolen in my life. What are you accusing me of?"

"You're an old con woman. You're lucky I'm not calling the police, now hand it over." He pursed his lips and cupped his hand towards her.

"Hand what...?" He reached for her jacket. She slapped his hand away and howled. "Don't you dare, you jobsworth. They pay you five pounds an hour to insult perfectly respectable members of the public? No wonder we're all going online now. I wouldn't steal the tat in here, moreover buy it." She pushed passed him, shoving her shoulder into his, and marched towards the door. She turned back to him, saw his shocked face and laughed. "Stick your putrid shop up your flaming arse."

"Well, look, if you're looking for somewhere to stay Kate, give me a call." Jennifer pushed a card with her phone number on it into Kate's hand as Flo sidled up between them.

"Who's this?" Jennifer twitched her nose at the old woman and stepped back. Kate felt a giggle rise, but managed to flatten it just below the surface. She felt exactly the same before she had gotten to know the old woman.

"This is Flo, I'm actually staying with her just now," explained Kate, pretending not to notice Jennifer's evident repugnance, but rather enjoying it anyway. "Anyway, Jenny, it was nice running into you. Bye." Jennifer watched as the two women flounced away and headed towards the river bend. When they were nearly out of sight, she leaned against the shop window and reached for her mobile phone. She punched an SMS into her phone. 'Found her!' She hit the send button and watched as the message disappeared from her screen. She walked along Argyle Street. The rain fell again and snaked onto her face and then off her chin. She was fortunate that when the torrent really began she was already nearly off the main track. Her phone vibrated in her pocket. Reaching for it, she headed into the subway station that operated in the central belt of the city. She could hear the sound of a guitarist who continued to play, despite the ailing weather. As she wiped her mobile phone and entered into her messages, she stepped onto the escalator and disappeared from sight.

7.

Bruce stood in the entrance of the police station and waited for Detective Inspector Morris to find time in his schedule for him. He was already annoyed that he had waited twenty minutes to be seen. On the second occasion that he asked the desk Sergeant how long this would take, he was met with a stony silence.

"Like that, eh?"

Morris finally slammed through the door at the exact moment that Bruce had decided to leave. He was grateful to see the man, even if he had a particular aversion to him, because he needed answers. Morris needed them more. He was escorted to a tiny interview room on a corridor that never seemed to end. He entered and took the seat offered to him by his host. It looked to him how he imagined solitary confinement would look in a prison. A light, wired to the ceiling, illuminated the bare green walls. It would be a test of endurance to spend more than twenty minutes in here, and Bruce joked to himself that he might confess all if he had to be locked in this room with the copper for one minute more.

Phil Morris was a tall man with wavy brown hair. Other than a fractured nose, he was quite nondescript, but not unattractive. He certainly wasn't in Bruce Anders' league. Nor did he want to be. Whilst Bruce wore bespoke suits direct from the tailors, Morris bought his off the rack at a department store. In terms of fashion, the two men couldn't have been further from each other. In determination and drive, the two were probably more alike than either would ever care to consider.

"You got that list for me?" Morris' tone was sharp now. It had been a long couple of days, and he wasn't in the mood for small talk or for any of Anders' cockiness. He took the list from Anders and perused the five names that had been scribbled onto the page. The first four didn't really stimulate any reaction. It was the final fifth name that intrigued him most. "Kate Mulgrew? Describe her." His interest in the last name wasn't lost on Bruce who lifted his eyelids just in time to catch the Detective's eyes peering over the page.

"I dunno Detective, about five foot four. Good looking. Skinny. Long dark hair." The description could have covered five thousand girls walking through Glasgow right now, but it didn't sound unlike the girl he had met under the bridge. It also fitted with her assertion that she was hiding out after a fight with her boss. He hadn't believed a word of it when she had spoken, but now he figured it might be true. Sometimes things are so damn simple that they transpire to be true.

"What happened with her?" Morris gazed intensely at Bruce until the man felt that he had no choice but to answer.

"She was a flake. She didn't want the work, she just wanted the money. She upset customers and other members of staff." He paused momentarily, running his fingers across the table. He looked nervous, Morris thought.

"She didn't want to have sex?" It was a cheap shot, but he wanted to gauge the reaction.

"We weren't offering sex, Detective. I've already told you that. Am I going to need my lawyer for your questions?" Bruce looked unnaturally angry, and Morris wondered exactly what nerve he had touched.

"No, just making sure that nothing was going on that shouldn't have been." His smile widened then, which unnerved Bruce further. "So you had a bit of a fight?" Bruce nodded but didn't speak. "What happened after that?"

"Nothing, I sacked her, and she left." Phil Morris tried to judge whether Bruce was being entirely forthcoming with him. Something seemed absent. A little grain of truth lay in what he was saying, but it was whirling in a vat of half-truths and lies.

"And when was that?"

"A few days before the fire. She threatened to destroy my club and said that she would kill me." He looked up, and Phil could sense the calculations going on in his brain. He already suspected that Kate Mulgrew had started that fire, Phil realised, and he was already planning to enact his own revenge. Phil knew instantly that Kate Mulgrew would be in severe danger if Anders managed to get to her before he did. A man like him didn't take too kindly to somebody interfering with his business. Certainly not burning it to the ground. Was he being completely truthful, Phil wondered? It seemed too convenient that he was suddenly telling him about Kate and her threats now. Why not mention it when they had met the day before? Surely a death threat wasn't something a person would forget that quickly.

"And you're sure this is everybody?" Bruce flinched. It was fleeting, but long enough for Morris to catch it. "What aren't you telling me, Mr Anders?"

"Nothing Detective, I've co-operated as much as I possibly can, but I'm becoming tired of your accusations. I thought I was here to help with your enquiries." The two men locked eyes then, staring at each other just long enough to unnerve the other.

"You are, and I appreciate it," he lied, "If you can think of anything else, call me." Bruce nodded and stood up to leave. As Phil escorted him to the reception area, an awkward silence developed between them. Finally, when they got to the final set of doors, Bruce turned to Phil.

"Do you know who the girl was in the fire? You know, the body?" He couldn't say the word 'dead'. That wasn't lost on Phil Morris who, up to now, had been perturbed by Bruce's lack of concern for the person who had died.

"How do you know it was a girl?" His lips were upturned even more now. He was playing with Bruce. Bruce knew it and felt himself being pulled into a mental game of snakes and ladders. He would regret his answer later, because without really realising what he was saying, the words tumbled from his tongue.

"I don't hire rent boys, Detective."

8.

As Kate followed Flo back to the river bend, she chattered infectiously. Flo saw genuine laughter in her eyes and it changed her face completely.

"Did you see the look on her snooty wee face?" Flo had asked almost immediately when they had left Jennifer behind. Kate had, and she was ashamed to admit it was much the same as her own reaction when she had first met Flo. However, the hours with the old woman had been like music to her soul. She had started to escape from her self-absorbed despair and had initiated a conversation about her life, about why she was on the streets, and about why she couldn't go home. Flo understood perfectly why Kate wouldn't go home. Every person who ended up on the streets had something that they were running from, even if it were just themselves.

Flo unburdened her shoulder of her bag and sat down upon it. After spending all day on her feet, it was like a velvet cushion on her bony backside. She pulled a bottle of gin from inside her massive pocket and called to Marv to come over to her. The old man grumbled to himself and then lurched towards Flo and snatched the bottle from her hand. In the hours that Kate had been with them, she still hadn't heard Marv speak. Then, Flo patted the other half of the bag and invited Kate to sit beside her. All the tension that had initially existed between them had long since disintegrated. As she sat, Flo eyed Kate wryly.

"I know we were laughing about that girl Kate, but speaking seriously to you now..." Flo leaned in and Kate could almost taste her breath "... people like her are not to be trusted. I've been on these streets for longer than I can even remember, and people like her are bloodsuckers." Her voice rose emphatically as she pushed home her point.

"Thank you Flo. I can look after myself though." Flo smiled maternally and rubbed her hand across Kate's leg.

"I know you can, but you're sweet. And you're fresh. And there are people who will pick up on that immediately and they'll take advantage. It looks like somebody already has from what you've told me. So, I just want you to be prepared and to know that not everybody is like me. You stick with me, kiddo, and I'll look out for you." Kate felt a tug on her heart and she had the urge to hug the old woman. She really believed that Flo cared for her, and it was a strange sensation. The only other person who had ever come close to caring was her husband, and she had rejected him almost from the outset.

"Thanks Flo. I know you will, but I can't stay here and take advantage of your kindness forever." She had appreciated Flo letting her bed down, but she still had somebody who was out there trying to get to her. Eventually, they'd work out that she was here and, when they did, Marv and Flo would also be in danger. She didn't want to, but Kate knew that she was going to have to make a move very soon. She just didn't know how to tell Flo yet.

9.

"Donna, you wanna come with me?" Phil Morris waded into the staff room and recalled the comments that Bruce Anders had made. Mostly though, he felt growing trepidation for the safety of Kate Mulgrew. Anders had carved himself into the victim by weaving a sorry tale that had instantly incriminated the girl. Why though? According to Bruce, she had vowed not only to destroy his business, but to kill him with her own bare hands. It was easy to see that she was the most likely suspect. Of course, he suspected that Bruce Anders would likely have an endless list of enemies. Miss Mulgrew was probably the latest in a long line.

"Where are we off to?" Donna wiped away the remnants of a half-eaten lunch as he held up the scrunched piece of paper in his hands. It was the list of five names that Bruce had scribbled for him. Now, he would work his way through them in meticulous order until he cracked open every sordid detail of the club's business and Bruce Anders impervious nature. Donna narrowed her lips, dumping her sandwich on the plate, and following him into the hallway. He stormed through thick wooden doors, his temperament unusually fractured, and led her into the car park.

One by one, he drove to the addresses he had managed to acquire for each of the former employees that Bruce had forged rifts with. The only one he didn't have an address for was Kathryn Mulgrew, but he was sure he knew exactly where he would find her. The first three girls had either conveniently contracted amnesia or had made it quite clear that they wouldn't be speaking to the pigs. However Ashleigh Higgins, the fourth girl on the list, was somewhat more forthcoming. She was an emaciated girl with blonde curls that had been scraped away from a face that looked somewhat reptilian when she licked her lips, a tic that she had evidently carried with her since a young age.

"He's a pig. I'm glad somebody finally taught him a lesson," she had said petulantly when Phil Morris arrived. She had led them through a dank hallway in her shared accommodation into a sparse bedroom that was surprisingly bright and clean.

"How long did you work for Bruce Anders?" Donna led the way when she sensed that Miss Higgins was somewhat nervous in the presence of men.

"A few months. He doesn't keep people around very long. Only as long as they are useful to him. I learned very quickly that you don't get on the wrong side of him." Donna followed her gaze across the street where the grey Victorian facade of a derelict building blocked any natural daylight from coming in.

"Did he threaten you?" Phil Morris enquired, his voice cutting through the dim atmosphere.

"No, Bruce Anders doesn't threaten you. If he wants something to happen to you, he doesn't bother telling you. It just happens. You should ask Nicole Murray. Or you probably can't seeing as she was so frightened by him that she moved back to London." Phil's fear had grown with every visit as he thought about what would happen to Kate if Bruce Anders found her first. He thought about Ashleigh's words about things happening if Bruce Anders wanted them to happen. Could Bruce be responsible for the dead body in his building? Had he burned the place down himself, or arranged somebody to do it, so that he could conceal as much evidence as humanly possible?

"Were you afraid of him Miss Higgins?" Donna asked sharply.

"Physically? No! I have four brothers who have ten pounds each on that pig. If I wanted to have the shit beaten out of him, it wouldn't have been a problem. Look, Detective, I'm sure you know what kind of club HEELS is. Bruce Anders is no better than a street pimp. But I don't want my brothers to know what I did for a living. See, that's the hold the bastard has over you. So, no, I wasn't afraid of his threats of violence. I was more frightened of his threats of exposure." Donna nodded in acknowledgement.

"Miss Higgins, can I ask where you were between the hours of ten pm and midnight on the seventh of November?"

Phil Morris changed the course of the conversation. He was quite sure Miss Higgin's four brothers could do some damage if required. He also believed that she would do anything to avoid them knowing that she had been a hooker. Would that stretch to murder and arson?

"If I recall properly, and you can check with her, I was here with Ang from next door. That's Angela McCormack. She lives in the next room." Phil was sure her alibi would check out. He got the impression that she wished she had thought of burning the club down, her only regret being that Bruce wasn't locked up inside. She would probably have worn a t-shirt to advertise it. His instincts were generally very good when it came to picking out the real bona fide killers. She wasn't one. This would lead him to the final name on the list. Kathryn Mulgrew. Where did murder fit in on her radar? He was afraid now because he was becoming more certain that Bruce Anders' list was nothing more than a diversion. A diversion from what though? If Miss Higgins was right, Bruce Anders was not a man to be messed around with. What if Bruce Anders was a killer? What if Kathryn Mulgrew wasn't an arsonist or killer? What if she was simply Bruce Anders next victim?

10.
Flo watched with exasperation as DI Morris strode into her lair, intent burning in his usually calm eyes. He was followed by Donna Barclay who tipped her hand to Flo. It wasn't news to anybody that Flo treated the patch under the bridge like her house, and anybody else who slept there did so *only* with her blessing. Kate slept on the pile of clothes, catching a long awaited cat nap and seemingly oblivious to the police presence. She heard Flo mutter something to her and drifted into consciousness.

"I think this visits for you, Missy," the old woman said, speaking loud enough that only Kate could hear her.

"What?" Kate snapped awake and saw the DI approach. He was framed by the glow of a street lamp as dusk gave way to the chilling night time.

"Detective Morris, this is becoming a daily thing, what can I do for you?" The steam from Flo's plastic cup rose up and formed a halo around her face.

"Flo, I'm not here to see you. I know; you're shocked!" Flo didn't turn to look directly at Kate, but she saw her twitch nervously from the side of her eye. "Kathryn?" The girl looked as if she had just been caught in the path of an oncoming truck. Flo put a hand on her shaking arm to calm her.

"Don't worry, love. Mr Morris is one of the good 'uns." She turned back to the DI and eyed him suspiciously. "What do you want with her, anyway?" Kate stood up from the rags and dusted her skirt down. She felt her bowels shift and wondered if she might regurgitate the can of cold spaghetti that Flo had foisted upon her.

"What do you want?" Morris eyes hurtled up and down. She sounded a little sharper than she had a few days before when he had first met her. He wondered, and not for the first time, what the hell she was doing here. She really didn't strike him as somebody who should be on the street or somebody who would be selling sex for a living. He knew as well as anybody that desperate people did unthinkable things.

"I need to know where you were between the hours of ten and midnight on the seventh of November." Her mind tripped over the loop of thought as she tried to picture her movements prior to being followed. She couldn't think straight away. Anxiety crept upon her. She had barely slept. She was cold and hungry. Mostly, she was just tired of feeling so damn tired and afraid. She ran her mind back to that first night that she had realised somebody was following her. She then thought of her aimless stroll around the city as she cried herself in and out of every eventuality that she could think of. She had never felt so desolate. Now, she couldn't even remember exactly where she was, or when. She couldn't even remember what day that was.

"What's happened?" She finally found the words. She couldn't remember where she had been, and she didn't want to fabricate a lie, so she simply threw a question back at him. Flo watched with growing unease. This girl really might be in some kind of trouble. Trouble that Flo couldn't protect her from. Was it something to do with that fire that DI Morris had asked about, she wondered? She felt herself tense up and the muscle in her arms tightened and tugged. She had felt an affinity with Kate since the first moment they had exchanged a single word. Now, she could think of nothing but trying to help her.

"She was with me." Flo interjected, aware that she might be deflating the air from Morris' investigation. "All Night! Hardly the weather for being out and about now, is it Detective Morris?"

"So, why was it that I saw you at the top of Buchanan Street at eleven that night, Flo? ALONE! Let's try again, and this time, let the girl answer herself." Flo shook her fist at him and moved around her empty sack. Kate had no choice but to speak for herself now. She wasn't able to hide behind Flo and, if she were perfectly honest, she didn't think she should be, anyway. The old woman had been very kind, but nobody did anything for nothing. What price would she have to pay later? She moved towards the DI. He was struck by how attractive she was; beautiful in fact. Her face was masked in fading cosmetics and her hair was congealed to her scalp, but there was no denying that it veiled a girl too beautiful for these streets. He felt dejected then. Like the whole world was a melting pot, and he wanted to climb out.

"I can't remember." She smiled awkwardly, a gentle smile that he assumed was for the benefit of putting one over on him. He wondered if that ever worked.

"Miss Mulgrew, you told me the other day that you were here because you had a spat with your employer. It was a little more than that, wasn't it? Did you know that the club that burned down belonged to Bruce Anders? That was who you worked for, Miss Mulgrew, isn't it?" She nodded her head and looked at Flo. DI Morris continued. "Well, isn't it? Are you aware that we found a body, or at least part of a body? We'll really need you to account for that night, Miss Mulgrew." Flo looked anxious. She wanted to shake the silly girl. To tell her to come up with a lie, any lie, but not to just throw herself under the bus without even trying.

"I was sleeping by the side of the river," she offered, but was it too little, too late? "Flo kindly offered me a break from the rain."

"She's a regular Samaritan, our Flo," it was Donna's turn to speak now. Flo took a bow and stuffed a loose strand of hair back under her hat.

"Am I under arrest?"

"Not under arrest. You're simply helping me with my enquiries."

As Kate stood at his side, Flo moved around them. Her agility still surprised him. She had been out in the tumults of winter for as long as he had been on the force. She had aged so badly that he feared she was probably twenty years younger than she looked. Still, she was spritely enough, although her posture suggested that she was buckling from the unfeeling winters and the constant weight of her sack.

"Mr Morris. Do me a favour," she hissed at Donna. "Don't bring your entourage round my house again." He held the door open for Kate and watched her lower her body onto a leather seat. As DI Phil Morris pulled open the door on the driver's side of the vehicle, he tipped a salute in Flo's direction.

As the car pulled away, Flo watched the expression change on Kate Mulgrew's face. Through re-enforced glass, there was no mistaking the anxiety that washed across her eyes. Flo twitched furtively and watched the car disappear into the dark.

11.

As the car pulled away, and Kate disappeared from sight, Flo suddenly became aware of a man standing on the edge of the river. He watched her attentively, seemingly absorbing every groove in her face and crumble in her shack. She wasn't close enough to see him completely, and his face was partially cowering under shadows, but his stiffened stare made her shudder slightly. For one frightening moment, the rest of the world fell away, and she felt herself entrapped by his glare. She stepped back, so that she stood beneath the arch of the bridge and watched as he turned to meet his own reflection on the river. She leaned down, reaching slowly for a knitted scarf and felt a jolt; stronger this time; more savage. She did not dare look back up, for she feared he'd still be staring when she did.

Finally, after what appeared to be the endless flirtation between her fear and her determination, Flo looked back at the spot that he had been standing. He was gone. She stepped back out of the shadow and looked in every direction. He had disappeared almost as quickly as he had appeared. Who was he? Had they found her? Finally, after all these years, was somebody going to find out who she really was? She checked her own anxiety, plucking it from her tingling skin, and hid it away again. She thought about his face. Too many years had passed for her to really recognise a face from the past, but had she known him? In her previous life? There was something in the way that he stared so unfalteringly at her. As she rushed back to her piles of clothes, she clung onto the knowledge that it wasn't the first time that she had feared her past coming back to find her. Guilt was a sturdy, but fearsome, companion. So, she found a pocket in her mind, folded up the fear and the man and the knowledge of her past, and locked it away inside. She felt ridiculous then. Lots of men stood by the river. Lots of men got lost in thought and then curious about the people who were living under the bridge. Maybe he stared so intently because he had come down to this part of the river not realising that people lived here. Whatever the reason, he had disappeared without speaking to her, or flitting into her world. She felt mild relief then and brushed off the relentless disquiet that had forged its way into her. Whatever had gone on in the past, she was quite sure that she had left it behind. Too many years had passed for anybody to recognise her. To anybody with half an interest, she was just the crazy old lady who lived under the bridge. She was happy to keep it that way.

12.
Glasgow city centre was a bastion of multi-cultural existence that had once been a bleeding wall of hostility. Now, those who had once feared discrimination moved freely in the knowledge that Glasgow was coming to celebrate diversity. There were little factions in the outer reaches who still upheld the barriers of the less welcoming past. The city centre, however, was a haven of acceptance that even stretched an arm of friendship to the once fearful homeless community.

Kate stared out of the car window and wondered why she didn't feel entrapped. The door was locked, yet it felt very much like riding in the back of a taxi. Maybe she felt relieved after Detective Barclay offered to put the heating on, the bite of the cold firmly locked on the other side of the door. The car was black throughout, leather seats folding into the corners and meeting seamlessly with the black floors. A radio boomed to life as the car jerked to a stop at various junctures. The ride was slow and without event, and it was certainly not the experience one might expect when under arrest. Which, they had assured her, she was not.

The city centre, as they cruised through it, juxtaposed with the sedentary world that Kate had been used to before she had left her husband. As she smiled politely and offered minimal retort, she stared through the window, cutting a ghostly figure in a muddled fracas. When the small talk had passed, Phil Morris turned up the radio and hummed tunelessly to a Rihanna song that Kate barely recognised. She smiled, finding it refreshing, which met with a smile of approval in his rear-view mirror.

"You like this song?" He spoke gently as Donna frowned at him. "What?" He mouthed the word to her and saw her forced irritation. Then she smirked.

"Not really," Kate answered. "I really don't listen to modern music much."

"You like the classics? Meat Loaf, Fleetwood Mac, The Stones?" She thumbed her nose and then stifled laughter.

"Not that classic." He laughed gently, aware that Donna was eyeing him.

"Ah, so you must have grown up in the nineties then. Those guys think they invented music. Britpop and all that business. They borrowed the sounds of the old tunes, and now everybody thinks they're god's gift to songwriters." Donna rolled her eyes. However, when she looked back at Kathryn Mulgrew, she saw the girl shifting flirtatiously in the seat. She made for a pitiful sight; hungry and exhausted, yet she still had the nous to understand when a man wanted her. She wasn't as wet as she seemed. They finally pulled into the police station car park at just after ten p.m. and prepared themselves for a tiring night of interrogation.

13.
Peter Dow propped himself against the glass ledge of The Bridge Bar. A tussle had broken out a few moments before but had been swiftly dispelled by the bruise-happy landlord. It was a quiet Thursday evening in Glasgow and Peter had come here to drink away the cobwebs of his mind. There had never been a problem that Peter hadn't resolved with alcohol, yet he had managed to conceal his addiction for more than a decade. He had taken his first drink at fourteen and had embraced the levitation of the highs and the backlash of the lows without ever moving to the responsible state that many adults grow into. Even at his most inebriated, Peter could still recall his first drink. It was the day after his mother had walked out. In the weeks that followed, his father had climbed into mental decrepitude. *Like father, like son*; she had said on so many occasions. He had moved onto vodka during his four years of university before discovering the taste of finer things. Now, he balanced the stress of his victories with an enviable juggling act of distasteful sex, forty year old whiskey's and a mild dependency on both legal and illegal highs.

The air was filled with the sound of a dance CD, electronic beats that served only to carry one song into the next without distinction. Peter groaned balefully. The words from the article still blazoned through his head, hammering transiently with the ethereal sounds that filled the air. A body had been found. The guilt bathed through him like acid down a drain. Whose body had it been? The fire had been set late at night. Why was anybody even in the building after hours? The club closed at eleven p.m. He rested his forehead upon his hands and leaned forward. The room swirled defiantly, and he struggled to remain upright.

As if on cue, Bruce Anders casually entered the bar, and sauntered towards him. The man with no worries, it would seem, nothing fazed Bruce. Peter had often wondered just what his Achilles heel might be. He heard the thud of the cellar door behind the bar slam shut.

"Rum and coke please Archie, and whatever Mr Dow's having." Bruce was too smooth for comfort. There was something affected about the way he moved, about the way he spoke, even in the way he dressed. Peter had often mused about how he would love to strip away the layers and find that Bruce was just like everybody else; broken and decayed. Rotten from his core and outwards. Bruce would never let it happen. He had manipulated everybody and everything until they had found themselves at his supreme mercy.

They moved to a private booth in the corner of the bar. The music lowered and thudded in the gloom. Bruce's eyes followed the hue of red and blue and crystal bottles along the ledges of the bar. If his heart rate had lifted, he would never show it. Nor would he sweat, or cry or do any of the awful humiliating things that Peter, *the drunk*, had undertaken to do since his life had begun to unravel. He had mired in the walls of depression and he couldn't see the way back. Bruce had him firmly under his control, and whichever way he moved the pieces, he was at an absolute stalemate.

"I've just saw that little bitch Kate being taken away by the police?" Bruce finally spoke as he felt the sweet of the Rum and coke tingle on his tongue. Peter's eyes lifted spontaneously as the colour drained from his face. His mind twisted round the words of the article again. "DEAD BODY!"

"Why do they think she's involved?" He watched Bruce smirk as his upper body swaggered. His eyes were ablaze with malice and Peter suspected there was nowhere that girl would be able to hide, in jail or on the streets, where Bruce couldn't find her. Not under a single rock on God's green earth. He looked pleased with himself. As if he, himself, had pulled off the victory of the year.

"Because she did it Pete. She burned down my bloody club. It can't be a coincidence that I sacked her and then the place burns to the ground the very next day." He looked across the bar, cautiously searching the rows of revellers who just might feel the urge to listen to their conversation.

That's quite an assumption to make," Peter whispered, careful not to ignite Bruce's notorious spite. Bruce frowned in wonderment. Was Peter in the same conversation that he was in?

"A pretty fair one, I'd say, Pete." He laughed ruefully, and thought of all the other girls who had worked for him at HEELS? He had decided against omitting any names from the list. DI Morris would only find something to suspect him of if he hadn't been completely forthcoming. So, the little bitch's name was on the list. If she went to jail that wouldn't be the worst thing. There was more than one way to skin a whore alive, and he had as many girls on the inside as on the out.

"What are you going to do about it?" Peter looked nervous. He looked over his shoulder and searched the faces of revellers for anybody that he feared would be listening in on the conversation.

"I've got my contacts. Right now, I'll let that bloodsucker Morris have his fun. I hear he likes the younger ones. Once she's out of his hands, she's fair game." Peter chuckled anxiously, his mood becoming worse by the second. He couldn't put the fire out of his mind, nor that there had been a dead body in the rubble.

"Do they know who the body belongs to?" Sweat swept across both his brows now, and he used a napkin from the table to wipe it.

"Nope! They think it'll be days before they find out who she is." Peter felt his shoulders sag.

"She?" Bruce simply nodded his head and took a swig of his glass.

"How can you be so sure that Kate girl did it? She doesn't seem the type," he finally offered, scared that he would be implicated in anything more. He was sweating profusely now, the beads forming thick and fast and tumbling down his face like condensation in a heatwave. Bruce's anger finally tippled.

"She's a whore Pete. They're the type to do anything... and get away with it. She burned down my club for fucks sake. Why are you defending her, anyway? Is she your one?"

"My one," Peter looked confused, his eyes darting from side to side.

"You all have one. All your dirty little perverts." There was something jeering in his tone now. "That's it. She's your one. You come to the club, you meet her, and she seems different. She's beautiful of course. She looks like she really wants you. She'll laugh at your terrible fucking jokes. She'll see through your layers of fat and your drinking and the fact that you pay her half of what she's worth for a blow job. But she'll see what a decent kind man you are. After you've left, you'll think about how you'll rescue her, and she'll be so thankful that she never has to give another man a blow job for half her worth again. She'll be forever indebted to you. Eventually..." he paused menacingly "she won't even notice that you're turning into a middle aged blob with no hair and that you have the constant stench of alcohol oozing from your sweating pores." He paused, realising that his voice had risen to a level that was audible to some of the other drinkers in the bar. He turned to meet their eyes. "What the fuck are you looking at?" A timid man at the bar quickly averted his stare. He looked back at Peter who looked as if he might implode any moment.

"I never ever paid that girl for sex," he offered defensively. Bruce sniggered, a look of pity crossing over his bronzed face.

"Anyway, I'm not even here about that. What's going on with my casino permit?" Peter looked shocked as if he had just discovered another layer to the devil.

"Nothing, Bruce. We can't do anything about that just now. It's all over the news that your place was a brothel. Your name will be on every official desk in the city. If I push through a permit for you right now, questions will be asked." Peter fiddled with a beer mat, nervously avoiding Bruce's hardened stare.

"And if you don't, questions will be asked. I'll make sure of it." Even on his own tongue, Bruce felt sick from the sour taste of blackmail, but it was his last option. He needed that casino to go through. He had investments from other businessmen in the city, some even more dangerous than himself, and he couldn't contemplate delaying or losing the permit.

"You've got nothing. Anything you had on me has burned to the ground." Was Peter really that stupid, he wondered? Those videos weren't kept on the grounds; they were transferred to a hard drive and kept in a safe. Bruce wanted to tell him exactly what he had on him, but he decided to save that titbit of information for a time when he really needed it. For now, he needed his commitment.

"You seem very sure of that. You're willing to risk your career? Your reputation? Everything you've worked for?"

"Bruce, if your name is even highlighted at the moment, they're going to want to know how I know you." He was begging now; pleading that a last strand of decency existed between them. It only served to confirm to Bruce that the game was firmly on his side. Peter had no more moves. He decided to labour the point just a little more.

"And how you fund your campaign. And how you're the signatory on over a hundred major permits *with*, I might add, criminals who are looking to hide their money inside legitimate businesses in this city. How are you going to explain that your contacts list is a who's who of Glasgow's underbelly?" Bruce savoured Peter's discomfort. The man was at breaking point. It was written in the sweaty etches of his face, and Bruce danced in the certainty that Peter would risk the questions about their association over complete exposure. He ordered another drink for Peter before leaning over him. "Now get it together, Pete. Make this your last drink, eh? You won't be much use to me if you drink yourself to death."

14.
The beams of his investigation had collapsed just after one a.m. DI Phil Morris had stormed out of the interview room and demanded that somebody go to the Delmar Karaoke Bar on Hope Street. He had been seething at the ineptitude surrounding him when Kate finally announced that she had an alibi for the entire evening from the time she had entered the Delmar until the time she had, apparently, been tailed towards Flo's patch. It was fair to say that, upon meeting her, Morris was as convinced of her guilt as he was of Anders innocence. So, it was with mild relief that he had discovered that she couldn't possibly be guilty. However, it left him with more questions than answers. If only she had been able to remember her alibi two hours earlier, it might have saved all of them some time.

He looked at the young woman, no bark or bite, and actually felt genuine sympathy for her. She had been crying for more than half of the interview, and he hadn't even cranked up the pressure yet. She hadn't requested legal assistance, which he had offered twice, and he wondered if she even knew that she had a right to have an appointed solicitor present.

"Am I being charged?" she had asked, and it was the one time she hadn't seemed emotional or scared. He had left her to sob it out alone with a mug of hot steaming coffee. Within twenty minute he had her alibi confirmed. She had been thrown out of the Delmar on the night of the fire because she had been trying to steal drinks from paying customers and Stevie Wright wasn't having it on his premises. She had created quite a fuss and had to be virtually carried out by security. They kept a log of these things because you never knew when somebody would claim that they had been manhandled inappropriately by one of the security team. Wasn't that convenient, Morris thought pleasingly? At least for Miss Mulgrew.

"So, I'm free to go?" she stared at him with wide eyes and he felt himself melt slightly. She really was beautiful. Even with the fading make up, the unkempt hair and the slutty outfit, she was better looking than anybody he had seen in quite a while.

"Not yet," he said and pulled his eyes away from her. Donna wanted to intervene then. She knew of no reason to keep the girl here any longer. She looked at the girl's desolate face and then at Phil.

"But you said you're done with me and that my alibi checked out. You said that you believed me when I said that I hadn't burned his stupid club down." All of that was true, but he didn't feel right about dropping this girl off on the streets at this ungodly hour. So, he lied a little. He was as concerned for her fragile mental state as he was for her physical safety. He looked at Donna. Her apprehension hung vividly in the atmosphere of the room. She knew exactly what he planned to do, and she didn't like it one bit. It went against every procedure she knew of to lock somebody in a cell who they had already proven their innocence.

"I've got a few more questions for you, but you look done in, so I'm going to let you have a lie down and then we'll talk again. You probably don't even know what you know." She looked angry then, her expression switching between mild annoyance and outrage.

"You can't lock me up. I haven't done anything." If he heard her, he didn't acknowledge it.

"Detective Barclay, can you take Mrs Mulgrew to the holding cells please," then he turned back to Kate and smiled. "It's only for a few hours. I just have a couple of things that I'm not sure about, and I think it'll be better answered when you've got a clearer head."

As she stood in the door frame and gestured her into the hallway, she saw him stare at her.

"Why the hell are you sleeping on the street anyway? Don't you have family somewhere?" She lowered the lids of her eyes and eyed her skinny legs. She knew what she must look like because she didn't even recognise her own sad self. He had made her feel so easy when he spoke, his voice soothing and encouraging, that she wanted to open up the pyramid of lies that her life and become and bring it crashing to the ground. She felt an ache wash across her like a flowing tsunami, and she felt the urge to both scream and cry. Would it help her feel better? She saw herself in the mirror as she lifted her eyes again, and she felt contempt for the weak woman that she had become. She saw Morris shake his head as she was led into the corridor. When she was safely locked inside the holding cell, she finally felt her emotions cripple her. She bit on her lip and felt it fall out of her at every pore. She bit so hard that she almost tasted blood. Then, her calm restored, Kate fell back onto the filthy little mattress and tried to diffuse all the anger that reeled inside. Whoever it was that was following her, taunting and tormenting, she was sure that they would have to make their move soon. She didn't know their motivation. She didn't have any idea what their end game would be. When they struck, though, she had to be ready for them. Her only other choice was to lie down and die.

15.
Flo hadn't slept a wink the entire night. She couldn't get the image of that man standing by the river out of her mind. In addition to that, she had noticed that Kate hadn't returned. She looked into the invisible space of her mind, hooking onto the shelter of her own thoughts, and wondered what might have become of her if old Floozy Susie hadn't taken her under her wing. She might have roamed without fear and walked straight into her own undoing. If she had survived that long. Those who had found their survival instincts on the cold grey streets knew exactly how to devour those who hadn't, and probably wouldn't, find theirs. Kate seemed resilient, but she also seemed naïve and too damn trusting. A mistake Flo had never made, even before Susie had come along.

Flo felt sadness then. For the family she had left behind, for the self-degradation she had endured, and the damage she had unleashed to those people she had run away to hide from. Unbeknownst to her, most of it was merely an infraction of her conscience as she wandered the well-trodden path of misplaced guilt. She watched the river as it reached its highest peak in 20 years and she knew of all the dreams and hopes that must have drowned there. The Clyde was a beautiful beast, never-ending and bewitching, but it was also a carnivore of grief and guilt. Then, her thoughts moved full circle from the secrets of the river back to the unexpected appearance of somebody who she thought she recognised. The man had been watching from the moment Kate had been taken away. There was something malevolent about the way he stared, a cold hard fixation of his eyes on her face. The warmth that made her approachable had evaporated, and she had shuddered more than she could remember shuddering in her life. Not a lot made her fearful, but that man's burning stare had frightened the ever living daylights out of her.

As dawn broke, she stuffed everything she owned into her little bag and took half a left over sandwich over to Marv.

"Marv, I'm off out. I thought you might like this to soak up some of that booze." He snatched it from her hand and grunted. She made her way out into the freezing temperatures of the desolate centre. Some shops had begun to open but it would be another hour or two before they'd become busy. So, she took advantage of the understaffed counters and the cloak of invisibility that the empty stores gifted to her. She wanted to get something for Kate to wear. Something warmer than the tiny clothes she had found her in. The girl had been resistant to wear anything of Flo's, and she didn't blame her. Once upon a time, she hadn't looked like an old trout in a net. Once upon a time she would have thumbed her nose at the rags that festooned her shabby body. So, she forgave Kate's snooty decline, and guessed that she was likely a size ten. Size ten's, even the warmer items, were small enough to squeeze into her inside pocket. She thanked the god of shoplifters that the girl hadn't been the size of an elephant.

16.

For the last two hours, Kate had listened to the woman in the next cell scream so violently that she thought somebody had skinned her alive with a razor blade. She had become so disturbed by it that she had even touched the walls to confirm that they were solid and that nothing was getting through them. She had dreamed for the first few hours; a dream of her former life where she and her husband and her baby had been happy. Harry had only been a few hours old, and Kate smiled from the combination of unfathomable love and weary exhaustion from a fifteen hour labour. Hugh had smiled wildly as a camera flashed a dozen times. Not a new modern digital one, but one of those old spooler ones that gave you twenty seven photos and only if you never messed the first few up. It was the strangest dream, because Kate had never felt that kind of instant motherly pride, and her husband hadn't even been present for the birth of Harry. In reality, she recalled being numb, and then an overwhelming wave of terror because she feared that the child would suffer from the maladroitness that she had been blessed with from her own inept mother. Harry had deserved better. Even when she got over the post-natal depression, and the engulfing guilt, she still hadn't been the mother that she should have been. She would leave him crying for untold hours between feeds and nappy changes, and she would sit and cry in a corner of her lounge. When he became a toddler, their relationship had solidified a little more, but most of it had been a front for her husband who seemed to take to fatherhood in a way that made her ache with envy. She now wondered if that was why she was so desperate to get away. Maybe they reminded her of the chink in her armour. Her inability to love properly and to feel maternal towards a child that had grown inside her for thirty-nine weeks.

Kate was brought back to the now with a clattering bang. The light flickered, dimming and then re-igniting the unmoving shadow of her limp body against the corner of the wall. She had no urge to move now. Was this as good as it got? If they brought her breakfast now, she would think she was in a five-star hotel by comparison to what she had endured recently. A lumpy mattress was a welcome improvement on a pile of clothes that oozed the scent of urine from every crevice. She felt ungrateful even thinking it. The last days had only been manageable thanks to Flo and her tiny slither of kindness. This bed, though, was the most relief she had felt in weeks.

"You can't keep her in there without probable cause," the PC looked irritated. As if he were surmising that Morris had given a room away that they needed for another guest. In fact, when he had finally stopped interviewing Kate Mulgrew at three in the morning, he felt just sorry enough to throw her into a cell. It was better than throwing her out into the street in the knowledge that she could only return to that shabby spot under the bridge. To share a makeshift bed of smelly clothes with Flo. In reality, the spot wasn't even good enough for Flo, despite how enamoured she seemed to be with it. Flo was a diamond in the rust, but even she couldn't protect Kate from the ones who were mere crud in the blind. So he had decided to save a few questions for the morning.

"Just take her some breakfast and shut up," Morris waved his hand at the younger man. He had only managed to sleep for two hours before returning to work, so he wasn't in the mood for a lecture about rules and protocol. The girl needed a bed. He had found her one temporarily. He didn't know if he was softening in his old age, or if he was just arrogant in thinking that she didn't seem tough enough for the streets of Glasgow. One thing he did know, though, was that she didn't burn down that building. He had seen many reactions, and heard many lies, and he could quite confidently say that she was absolutely shell shocked when he told her the details of the fire and asked her about the body.

One thing that perplexed Phil Morris was the body in the fire. He was still working his way through Bruce Anders list of employees. Nobody had been reported missing, and he had managed to account for everybody on the list. So who the hell was it that had died in that fire? He would now be expanding his enquiries to those other employees under Anders' employ. He was also determined to get Anders himself on a charge. He had slipped up yesterday when he had asked about the girl's body. How had he known it was a girl? Because he didn't hire rent boys! His protestations about his club being a legitimate lap-dancing club had proven to be a lie. Morris was going to prove it.

Kate had barely touched her food when DI Phil Morris entered the cell. She sat barefooted on the mattress looking half the size of the girl he had taken in for interviewing the night before.

"You can't keep me here. I haven't done anything," she said defiantly, her eyes narrowed into angry slits. Her face bore the insolence of somebody who could take on the world, but her body looked lank and defeated. He pitied her in that moment. What cruelties had life thrown at her that had brought her to this point?

"I'm not," he said calmly. He could tell her that he had done her a favour, but he wasn't sure she was ready to see it that way.

"You haven't even read me my rights," she continued. However, her face softened now, and he no longer felt the drip of her resistance.

"You're right, but you're not being arrested, so there's no need to read you your rights," he offered solemnly. He wanted to tell her that he believed her then, but what could that possibly do other than to give her a 'get out of jail free' card. So he simply moved into the cell.

"So, why am I here then?" She looked irritated now, like he was reading her some kind of riddle that she couldn't quite fathom. What the hell was his game? Locking her up for the night when he didn't suspect her of anything? 'Why?' she wanted to ask. However, she sensed that somewhere behind that sombre exterior was a man who was kind and thoughtful and who really had wanted to help her. Just as he had promised during the two hour interview the night before.

"Just between you and I, and the bed of course, you were better off in here than on the streets," he finally admitted. She smiled then. He really had been doing her a favour.

"So you've locked me up to keep me off the streets. How very noble," she laughed. She was teasing him. He handed over her shoes so that she could finish getting dressed, and then he escorted her out into the booking in bay. He held up a single finger to quieten her until they had both moved into the outside car park.

"I'm not going to lie to you Miss Mulgrew. I believe you're in danger. Bruce Anders believes that you burned his club and, in doing so, killed somebody. I don't get the impression that he's a man who gives a shit about the person who died. But I think he gives a crap about the inconvenience and the loss of bottom line. There's no telling what he's capable of. So I would be remiss if I allowed you to walk out of here and back onto the streets..."

He paused and waved his hand jovially in front of his nose. It was a childish gesture that made her want to laugh, but she allowed him to continue instead "… I know a place that might have a room. It's a friend of mine who runs it."

"You mean a hostel?" He nodded. She flinched, just momentarily, but enough for him to see the fear creep across her eyes. "Oh nooo!" She stopped in front of his car and rested against the bonnet.

"Have you got a better option?" he demanded. She really didn't. The thought of returning to the streets, with the notable exception of a reunion with Flo, filled her with untapped dread. She thought of Jennifer then, but hadn't it been Jennifer who had told the police where she was? She wanted to ask, but plundering over the where's and why's of how she had gotten here seemed redundant now. This guy was throwing her a lifeline, one that she hadn't earned or deserved, but she would be damned if she would refuse it.

"Okay," she finally agreed and sank into the car. It felt nice to sit up front, rather than feel like a prisoner in the rear. She kicked her feet a little and mused over the simple things that made her happy. As he started the ignition, she wondered where exactly he was going to take her. Anywhere was better than Flo's 'house', Bruce Ander's brothel or even prison. She sighed loudly and, for a moment, felt all of her troubles drift trip into the atmosphere. Just for a moment, she felt real unmitigated happiness. She wasn't naïve enough to believe that it would last.

17.

He had tried to ring the number four times, and now Peter Dow had moved on from concern to consummate fury. What the hell was Dave King playing at? He hadn't delivered what Peter needed, and he was already two thousand pounds out of pocket. Dave was notorious for being unpredictable and, more importantly, unattainable. It made sense for him to keep a low profile, but usually a person did that after they had completed the job and collected full payment. There was two thousand pounds more sitting in Peter's safe, awaiting the switch. Peter was becoming more and more anxious. He thought about the fire, the dead girl, and the repercussions when Bruce Anders discovered exactly who was responsible for the fire. Peter's only defence was that he had not ordered the fire. He simply wanted the documents and the videos that could potentially end his career. Every time he thought about the whole sorry mess, he perspired until his clothes clung to his skin. He didn't know how much longer he could go on without breaking. He was not a murderer. That he would be implicated in the death of a young woman was out with the realms of his thinking. He could not equate it with himself.

    The phone screamed to life again. He made a fifth, and final, call to Dave King.

    "Dave, its Pete here. Answer your bloody phone, will you? I need to find out exactly what you found in that building."

18.
"So where do you come from originally," he kept his eye firmly on the road, his brow furrowed in concentration. Kate shrugged her shoulders before wringing her hands through her hair. She longed to climb into a bath and scrub away the wreckage of her life. The silver Volkswagen cruised along the city streets, and she felt herself truly relax for the first time in months. Some rocker from the seventies droned from the radio, his husky voice filling the airwaves and the back end of the car.

"I'm not from Glasgow," she finally retorted, and felt him glance in her direction. He had seen every tactic of evasion known to man. Hers wasn't even a particularly good one.

"Okay, you got a family?" He wasn't giving up. He was a typical detective, always on the nose, scrambling about for every titbit of information on the people he came into contact with. Perhaps he hoped to find something that would solve his case. Maybe she would drop some innocent bombshell and blow the case wide open for him. Right now, she couldn't figure out what that might be. As she had persisted in saying during her interview the night before, if she had any information, she certainly didn't know it. Was he offering her a lift in the hope that she would open up and give him something that he could use?

"No," was as much as she could muster. Right now, she didn't feel like she had a family. Her mother was dead, her father absent and her husband and son most probably existing quite happily without her.

"Hmmmm!" He sounded doubtful, and she wondered if he had actually done a search on her. He probably knew her entire background. Was he too polite to say? Maybe this was all part of his game plan. She felt the shift as he moved into third gear and sped around a charcoal Mercedes. She admired the car, and the man who drove it, whilst touching the soft leather material that now clung to the skin of her thighs.

"I was married and had a kid...." The words circled in her mouth for less than a fraction of a second before dropping into the air. She didn't know why she had suddenly said it.

Maybe it was because she had nothing to hide. Maybe it was because she wanted someone, *anyone*, to know her. To know that her life hadn't been a kettle drum of emptiness.

"They still around?" His tone was offhand now, his focus on the M8 as the car cruised into the appropriate lane.

"Yeah, they're still around, but they don't want to be around me." There was a petulance to her voice, and he sensed that she hadn't walked away, but been forced to walk away. What exactly had happened to her to force her to walk away from her husband and her kid?

"That stinks," he merely offered in the wake of no more information.

"Not really. It was my choice. I wasn't the mother I was supposed to be, y'know. Failed at school, failed at marriage, failed at being a mum. Couldn't even keep a job for longer than a month. I don't think my husband liked me very much. He was probably sick of having to prop me up." He felt a tiny ache for this young beautiful woman who had moved past self-pity and now wallowed in the despair of feeling completely worthless. It was painful to listen to because he knew all too well the feeling of not being good enough. He had also spent his adult life hindered by self-doubt, thanks to the war zone that he had grown up in. He looked out the window and admired a black Porsche that sped by.

"Did he have a choice?" he finally asked. Kate shrugged guiltily. "It sounds to me like you're pretty hard on yourself. I mean, did your husband tell you he was unhappy, or that he wanted you to leave?" He waited patiently for her to answer. She didn't. She pulled her knees to her chin and watched him pull across two lanes and back up onto the city streets. "Look, not everybody is cut out for domestic life. I mean, I was engaged to a girl..." she turned now, curiosity passing over her elfin features, ".... hmmm yeah, exactly. Even me! I couldn't hack it, so I got out. She was the best person I could ever have imagined spending my life with. But I let my petty jealousy's come between us and eventually she walked out on me."

"So you're the jealous type?" she asked, casually. She had been with somebody like that once upon a time. Her husband, Hugh, had been the opposite. She would have longed for him to be the jealous type, or to show any reaction if somebody even gave her a second glance.

"Not generally. But when you're the ordinary one in the relationship and you constantly feel that you're punching above your weight, it eventually grinds you down." His voice was fused with bitterness, and it was the first time she had truly seen real anguish across his face. "She deserved better, so when she came back and offered me another chance, I told her no." Kate was surprised. He wasn't so different to her, she realised. She had left Hugh because she hadn't felt good enough. Hugh had begged her to stay. It was her who had walked out. Just as Phil had done with his former girlfriend. To find somebody who was cut from the same cloth as her made her feel slightly more human. She wasn't this monster that she had built in her own mind. Or, maybe he was just as much a monster as she was. Too monsters cruising off the hard shoulder and sharing the cruelties they had bestowed on the unintended.

"And I'm too hard on myself?" Phil's face flushed as she arched an eyebrow, and he recoiled from giving too much away. She saw his discomfort and looked away. A side effect of being a monster. "You're probably not as bad looking as you think you are."

"You haven't seen me in the morning." The awkwardness was broken by the injection of humour, and she laughed. It was a full hearty laugh that sounded like it had been locked away in a tower until the dragon had been sleighed and allowed it to break free.

"Yes I have, I'm seeing you now, aren't I?" He forgot it wasn't even afternoon. He had interviewed her until three a.m. Then, he had been back at the station a few hours later. So, she really had seen him at his most sleep deprived.

"So, what's the deal? You mentioned that somebody was following you the night of the fire?" There it was. The moment where he turned their casual banter and mild interest into an interrogation, she thought. She had mentioned being followed, and that she now suspected it wasn't the first time. They hadn't really touched on it again during the interview because she sensed that he thought it was a diversion to distract him away from the subject of the fire. She was apprehensive now. Should she open up to him? Could she trust him? He was, after all, just a copper who would arrest her in a heartbeat if he suspected that she was guilty of something. Luckily for her, the manager of the bar she had been thrown out of remembered her trying to steal drinks and some left over chips from a table during the time the fire had probably been started. She was innocent. She knew it, and she was glad that everybody else would.

"I don't know. I've just had this sense for weeks. A sense that I was being watched. At first, I thought I was just being paranoid, but then when I lived at that hostel I told you about, I saw somebody sitting outside in a car. I closed the curtain, and when I looked again, they were gone. Then I think it was the same car that night by the river that I told you about. When Flo found me on the ground. The first time I thought I was just imagining it, but this time the car was most definitely following me." She trembled slightly now, grasping one hand in the other, and he leaned over and rubbed her arm.

"Well, we'll get you somewhere safe."

19.

"I'm really sorry, they've got nothing for you," Phil lowered himself back into the car. They had been round three different hostels throughout the afternoon, and every place was filled beyond capacity. Short of throwing a spare mattress on the floor of the common room which would be a breach of health and safety, there was nothing any of them could do. "They said the best way to get you placed somewhere is for you to register with the homeless team."

"I'm not doing that. I know how that works. They'll call my husband, and he'll say that I can go home, and they'll say I'm not priority." She looked defeated now, like he had filled her with hope and then, at the last moment, snatched it away again. In reality, she didn't blame him at all. Who else would have spent the afternoon searching for somewhere safe for her?

"Would that be such a terrible thing?" He leaned round in his seat and faced her directly. He could see the shift in her expression.

"He'd feel obliged, he'd take me back because that's the kind of man he is. How can I do that to him and to Harry?"

"Harry?" The mention of her son's name seemed to soften her slightly.

"My son, I can't have him resent me the same way that I resented my mother." Ah, her mother again. He wondered if all of her pain stemmed from that one person. He had his own issues with his mother, but he loved and respected her, even though he knew her flaws.

"Your relationship wasn't good?" The question hung in the air for a moment while she contemplated just exactly how she would phrase her answer.

"It wasn't. She was a first-class bitch." Even if he could relate to it, it still sounded harsh.

"Ouch! But she's not around now?" She nodded her head again, and for a second it looked like she might cry.

"She died ten years ago." Her mother was dead, and yet she still harboured this intense dislike and resentment towards her. Phil was no psychologist, but he guessed that her mother must have been a real piece of work. How does a grown woman with her own family allow a dead parent to umbrella her entire life to the extent where she has to run away?

"I'm sorry."

"Don't be. Best place for her." She stifled a giggle then, like she knew that what she was saying might be a little wrong, but that she still thought it funny.

"Was she really that bad?"

"Yeah, she was cold and cruel. I never felt that I could measure up to what she expected from me. It was okay for her to have these expectations, but then she would bitch about everybody's expectations of her. How she was entitled to this and entitled to that." The atmosphere was dripping with hatred. Not the kind that most kids felt for a parent that might have left too early, or who was overcritical. A real loathing that he usually only saw from families of murder victims or parents of abused children. "She didn't really want kids, if the truth be known. I was an unhappy accident, and she spent every day letting me know it."

"What about your father?" There had been no mention of him so far.

"What's that?" She laughed, this time louder, and shrugged one shoulder childishly. "I never knew who he was." The pain burned her face now. She had just unloaded a lifetime of hurt in a few minutes, and he sensed that it wasn't easy for her to talk about. She had fastened her seatbelt again and wrapped her arms defensively around her chest. She was closing down. That was the price to pay for allowing somebody to crack you open. He felt sorry now. Had he been too pushy? Too assertive? He had to get her somewhere to stay, but as dusk began to roll around again, he realised nothing was going to get done for now. He couldn't turf her out onto the street. Not into the hands of Bruce Anders. Or, if she were lucky, a quick death from the throes of winter.

"Well, listen, if you can't go back home, and we can't get you a place tonight, then I'm going to have to take you back to mine." She looked surprise. She also looked apprehensive.

She moved back until she was almost touching the door window.

"You can't do that. What would your boss say"? It was a different response from what he expected. If she were going to say no, it was because he thought she might think it was inappropriate. She was showing the tiniest slither of concern for him, and it shocked him. Most people he had encountered on the streets would have taken his last quid from him. Not because they were bad people, but because they had so few choices. He had already ascertained that she wasn't typical of the people he had encountered on the streets. It only made him like her more.

"I don't know what she'd say, but I'd say it was none of her business." He smiled reassuringly. "You're not a suspect in any crime. You had an alibi. Christ, you had a real bona fide alibi, and you even had a fake one that transpired to be half true. We've nothing to hold you on," she laughed again, this time the hearty laugh that he had only heard once. "You've got no place to go and I have a spare room. In fact, I'm doing longs this week, so you'd actually be doing me a favour."

"How so?" She looked perplexed now. How would she be doing him a favour? She saw the grin across his face and waited for what was coming next.

"Walk my dog."

20.

"Who's there?" Flo stirred from her sleep so suddenly that she forgot exactly where she was. For a fleeting moment she wasn't the woman who lived under a bridge. She felt irritation as she was roused from the pleasure of a long overdue slumber. Marv still hadn't surfaced and, although he barely spoke or made a sound, she still missed the company and the security of having a man around the place. Although living on the streets meant having no real concept of time, Flo still wondered what time it was now. She felt discombobulated; like she didn't know if it was day or night. She had been woken with a start. Something had surprised her. Her eyelids drooped as she sat up on the makeshift bed, sifted through her rags, and crooked her head in the direction of the noise. She stood up, anxiety still roaming just below the surface. The ground was wet from flights of rain being carried in on the wind and her clothes felt damper than the norm. Sirens wailed in the distance, ferrying the Saturday night traffic of violence from the city to its nearby emergency departments. Then she heard a crack; the sound of leather meeting the tarmac, or the sound of somebody lurking just around the corner. Somebody was there. She couldn't see them, but she felt them, and there was no disputing what she had heard. Her body was frail, but her hearing and her mind were as sharp as they had ever been.

"Show yourself," Flo demanded, the quiver in her voice defying her bravery. She stepped forward, hushing the rampant voices in her head. She peered round the corner and felt the urge to run. Her old legs wouldn't carry her quickly enough, so she had no choice but to stay and flesh out her prowler. He moved so quickly she wouldn't have had a chance to flee. Instead, she screamed, a piercing scream that poked a hole in the air. She threw up her arms, her heart thudding in her chest so vibrantly that she thought that it might crash through her ribs. Then, he was upon her. Heaving and gasping as he gripped his arms

"Marv, what the hell are you doing?" He unleashed an ungodly aroma of stale alcohol from his breath, and she felt herself sicken at the scent. His eyes had surpassed their usual bulging hue of red and had turned a tinge of lilac. He mumbled something about sleep and fell past her. She reached for his back, her blackened talons resting upon his worn out duffle, and pushed him gently towards his pile of cardboard. She still had the adrenalin rushing from her heart to her head as he fell into a state of heavy unconsciousness. She felt relieved to have him back. She looked down upon her oldest companion and felt glad for his company. She wondered if Kate would be joining her. She looked onto the river; deep and wilful and thought how little she knew about Kate Mulgrew. Flo wasn't a particularly nosy person. She had learned that on the street you tell people what you want them to know. However, even she would occasionally be bitten by the bug of curiosity. As she turned back towards her bed, she suddenly found herself face to face with somebody she vaguely recognised. Their eyes flashed in the dark; brutal and wicked.

Flo looked defiantly as a grin spread across the ashen face. Then, her eyes widened as she saw a hand rise and reflect against the light. The fingers had turned a light purple as the hand tightened around a mahogany carving knife with a curved blade. Flo saw the terror in her eyes reflected back at her, her expression betraying the boldness that had so long been her reputation. As her fear consumed her, she heard a voice from beneath the hood. As she placed her right thumb upon her lips, she grabbed her crucifix with her right hand. When it was evident that she would never speak, the curved blade plunged through the layer of clothes. A scream lay just below the surface. The pain that followed was like nothing Flo had ever felt before. She felt the cold blade as it was inserted into her stomach several more times. Blood splattered as she fell back onto her pile of clothes and crumpled sleeping bag. If Flo wanted to scream now, it was probably too late. She lay there in the only place she had called home in ten years and heard the crack of the blade snapping from the mahogany handle. The blade itself remained rooted inside of her.

When Florence finally succumbed to death, it wasn't the dramatic finale to her life that she might have expected. Instead, it had been quiet and agonisingly painful. Long bloody gashes lay across her stomach but were concealed by various strewn fabrics that now dripped flesh and blood. A single stream of tears had rested in the crow's feet of her left eye. She had heard talk from people who had survived terrible violence that their lives flashed before them as they nearly died. That must have eluded Flo because she simply died, unobtrusively and without the fight that she would have hoped to put up. She ultimately focused her last thought on the son that she had not seen since the one terrible night where she had fled a terrible accident that had left a young man dead.

21.

Kate devoured a cheese sandwich, which was as much as she could hold down. Phil had almost forced her to eat it after she barely touched breakfast and refused his offer of lunch at various junctures throughout the day. It was just after ten p.m. and she sat on his sofa and looked around the pathetic lounge. It was not the grand affair one would expect from a salaried detective, but rather a gaudy throwback to the seventies where none of the furniture or décor matched. The one thing that she had gotten right when she had lived with Hugh and Harry was that she had an eye for style. Her house had probably meant as much to her as her marriage and being a mother. If not more! Now, she looked at the ugly brown canvas that adorned his feature wall and cringed slightly. She felt ungrateful for having such a thought. She took a drop of water from her glass and felt the cold freshen her drying throat. His mobile phone sprung to life then. He whispered an apology and explained he had to take it. Then he moved into the kitchen. She could hear his voice slightly, but couldn't determine what he was saying.

"I'm sorry; I have to go to work." When Phil came back to the lounge, she was rubbing the head of his border collie; a large black and white dog who then rolled onto his back and threw his legs up. "He likes you," he laughed, but it sounded forced. She looked up at his face, grey and stony and wondered what was wrong. Evidently, something work related had happened to shake him and she didn't feel that it was appropriate to ask.

The lights of other cars were jolting in the dark as Phil raced towards the river bend. He had felt sick since the news came through that the old woman was dead. He had known Flo since he had been in this job and she was one of the many homeless people he had taken food to over the years. She had also given him a few knees up if something had taken place nearby that she didn't like.

Her body lay like a ghostly shell, the arteries of her stomach poking out from under the entwine of her rags. Her corpse had begun to grow cold and, thanks to the frigid winter temperature in Glasgow, rigor mortis had already made a start on her greying skin. The red spray of blood had dried on her face, her eyes stared out into the whitening sky, and her lips crept back to reveal her decaying teeth as she had evidently fought for that final breath.

The murder crime scene had been preserved prior to DI Phil Morris' arrival. There was little doubt that Flo had been murdered where she lay because blood was spread across the ancient bricks of the bridge. The entire surrounding area had been cordoned off and lights had been instituted over the scene so that the attending officers and forensic team had access to as much of the grounds as required. Marv had been removed, having discovered Flo only minutes after her death, and placed in the back seat of a police car where he continued to sob and shake violently. Morris waved gently to him as he snatched a pen and signed his name against a register of attending personnel. Several other officials had signed in and had attended to Flo, from the departing medics to the forensics who now climbed into the tent that had been erected over her freezing body.

"Has anybody else had access to the scene prior to the paramedics?" Morris spoke directly to his partner Detective Donna Barclay, who also loomed over the body with a look of disgust that could have curdled custard.

"Only Marv, and I don't think he's been sober enough this year to murder anybody." As they made their preliminary walk through of the scene, Phil felt the urge to lean down and rub her arm, a last remnant of human dignity. He refrained and focused his sight on her wounds and then the sea of blood that veined around her corpse.

"It certainly looks like she was killed here," Donna noted, agreeing with Morris' initial assertion. "There's no attempt to stage it, and nothing suggests that the killer made any attempt to mislead us." It was something, he supposed, as he listened to his colleague verbalise his internal thought process.

"Who would do it, Barclay?" He thought about all the people who had probably come into contact with Flo over the years. She was a salt of the earth type. He didn't know why she was on the street any more than he knew why Kate Mulgrew was on the street. As he thought of the younger woman, it suddenly struck him that she had been in direct contact with two people who had died this week. She had also spoken of somebody following her. A puzzle unlocked itself in his mind as he realised that the girl could very well be in danger. Why had somebody burned down a lap dancing club that she had just been sacked from? Why had an old woman who had lived on the streets for years without incident, suddenly been murdered days after she took the girl into her confidence? Two pieces of the puzzle clicked together, but there was another hundred pieces that hadn't yet found its place.

"Who knows? I can't think of anybody who held a grudge against Flo." She looked down at the old woman's sunken face, the rigidity of her body and she felt a pang of fury. The distress across Flo's features also brought no comfort to either of them. She was benumbed of her misery now, carried away from the icy winds and hatred of a world that neither Phil nor Donna felt was good enough to have her. Now, death had seized her, carrying her lively character from the ravages of life into the quiet storm of other worlds.

It was difficult to know where the stench of the river ended and the scent of death began. However, both Donna and Phil wafted away the ugly fragrance on more than one occasion. It was so pungent and strong that Phil could actually feel it attack his nostrils. He wanted to lean into the river and vomit his guts out. The pathologist arrived shortly afterwards and allowed the two detectives to make a welcome retreat.

"Hey Phil. Donna. So, Phil, do you think this is related to your murder case up at that lap dancing club?" It was curious that both women had read his mind. He really did think there might be a connection between them both, and yet he couldn't fathom what that connection was. Surely it was only coincidence that Kate had been involved with both people who had died. However, there was no connectivity in terms of motives or method. It didn't make sense yet.

"Hi Carrie. How are you?" It was Donna who spoke back first, tucking her hair behind her ear.

"Good, good. I hope neither of you have contaminated my scene. How's the babies, Donna?" Donna smiled and nodded. This was usually the moment she would pull her wallet from her pocket and throw it open to reveal the toothless smiles of her little bundles of joy. Not that they were giving her much joy just now. Between teething and alternative sleeping patterns, she couldn't remember the last time she had a decent two-hour run at it.

"They're great, will have you round soon. It's been ages." Carrie smiled and stepped into the tent, the sound of her soft plastic shoes crunching against the tarpaulin mat.

"I'll go and check on Marv," Donna moved away from Phil and left him standing on his own. He looked up towards a nearby footbridge and saw hi-vis reflectors flash under construction lights. What were they doing up there at this time of night, he wondered? As he moved out from under the arch, he saw Donna put her arms around Marv and aided him in lifting his polystyrene cup of tea to his lips. He approached them both and saw the old man quiver under a mohair blanket.

"You okay, Marv?" The old man stared through bloodshot eyes, and Phil instantly saw the distress in his face. He understood completely. Marv had just lost the closest thing to family he had probably known for years. Flo was his street wife. They were bound together, not by marriage, but by solidarity and a genuine affection for each other.

"No," the old man answered, honestly. He no longer sat in the back seat of the police vehicle but had moved as close to the barrier as Donna would allow him. She continued to rub his arms from behind, offering him the comfort that not many other people would. Phil thought about Kate again. It was strange how he had gone from thinking about her as a person that he had to eliminate from his enquiries to a very real human being who he would have to break this terrible news to. He looked back at the flashing lights from under the bridge, then up to the nearby footbridge. Somebody who was working up there might have witnessed exactly what had happened to the old woman and, if they did, he'd be locking up the killer sooner rather than later. Donna watched him disappear up through the embankment of the river and onto the footbridge and wondered what the hell he was playing at.

22.
"Hello." The phone had rung for an inordinate amount of time and Kate was about to hang up. She had caught her breath and then felt it fall away again more times in the last ten minutes than she thought possible. Now, she heard the voice at the other end. He cleared the sleep from within his throat. She had woken him up.

"Hellllooooo?" It hadn't changed. It was still the same flat interminably boring voice that she remembered. She longed to say something. To offer some glimmer of hope. She remembered what she had said to Phil in the car today. If she asked him to have her back, he would. That was the type of man that he was. At what price though?

"I know you're there. I can hear you breathing." She gasped. She desperately wanted to say something; *anything*. Instead, she slammed the phone down onto its rest and felt the urge to cry. There couldn't be any tears left. She must have used every last one, and yet more came. Thick flowing streams that sat upon her lashes until she blinked. Musky climbed up onto the sofa again and rested his two front claws on her folded legs. She cupped her hand across his wet nose and rubbed. He whined contentedly. He shifted as she stretched her legs across the sofa and, together, they both drifted into a light short nap.

23.

Phil stepped onto the footbridge and felt the heightened lamps burn his eyes. He walked towards the man who had been watching the entire scene unfold.

"Excuse me, Detective Inspector Morris; I just wanted to ask you some questions about a crime that has taken place under the bridge. I wondered if you had seen anything prior to the police getting here?" The man looked startled. Had he been so engrossed with the events under the bridge that he hadn't noticed Phil walking towards him? Perhaps he was in shock?

"Sure. It was me who called the police." Phil hadn't been told who had called. Only that an emergency call had been made about a homeless person being assaulted. Strangely, Phil hadn't given it another thought beyond his thinking that Marv must have been the one to make the call.

"I see, well thank you. So you saw what happened?" Phil looked down at the arch of the bridge. It wasn't the clearest view, even with all the lights now surrounding it, but he could see well enough to have reasonable sight.

"I saw most of it yeah," he noticed that the man looked flushed and as he moved closer, he could smell alcohol from his breath.

"Are you working here tonight? It's a bit late to be doing work on the bridge at this time of night, eh?" The man nodded and tightened his grip on the bridge fence.

"I'm night watch. Security, really," he seemed shaken, although Phil wasn't surprised if he had just witnessed somebody being murdered.

"Okay, Sir, can I take your name." Phil pulled his pad from his pocket.

"Adam McGuigan."

"Your date of birth? And address?" Adam answered both questions quickly and watched as Phil scribbled the answers on to his notepad.

"Right, Adam, so can you just tell me exactly what you saw." Adam pulled his mobile phone from his pocket.

"I don't need to tell you, I can show you." Phil's eyes widened, and he felt his stomach tighten with the giddiness of a ten year old at his first football match.

"You have a photo?" Adam shook his head.

"No, I recorded it as soon as I saw that something was happening." Phil smiled then. He watched as Adam tapped into his phone and found the video. Phil stood on the footbridge and watched the four minute video of the old woman being savagely murdered. Against all of his expectations, there had been little fight. He also didn't know what the verbal exchange was. All that he knew was that a woman in a hooded top had entered into Flo's domain and killed her without protest. He felt the urge to scream at Flo then. Why the hell didn't she fight back? Why didn't she give the woman what she wanted? She was a stubborn old crow, and he felt sure then that she had paid the price with her life.

"Can I Bluetooth this to my phone? Can you show me how?" The younger man nodded and held a phone in each hand. Phil couldn't see the woman in the video well enough to identify her, but he was quite sure that a more tech-savvy colleague would be able to help. He had taken this one personally, and he knew it. He looked forward to staring face to face with the bitch that had done this. He thanked Adam McGuigan and made the short walk back to Donna. She was the only one he would share the video with for now. Tomorrow, though, he would begin the search for Flo's killer and wouldn't stop until he personally locked her up.

24.

Musky whined feebly in his sleep as he buried his nose under his paws. The sound of his laboured breathing had woken Kate up. He was an old dog, by all accounts, and she wondered just how many years he had been Phil's companion. She thought back to the time where she had acquired a dog, and it was the happiest time of her childhood. He was a decrepit border collie who had followed her home for a week. Finally, when her mother hadn't noticed, she had snuck him into her bedroom. It had taken less than an hour for her mother to hear the whimpering as she had tried to quieten him in her bedroom. Her mother had raged, as she did so often, and called for a local kennel to come and take the dog away. "It will have fleas," she had shrieked, with all the neurosis that Kate had come to know daily. Now, she realised that she hadn't particularly loved the dog, just as she hadn't ever particularly loved anything or anybody. He was a representation of something that would just be hers. Like everything else, her mother had devoured it, ensuring that Kate continued to have nothing and nobody.

Kate sometimes saw her mother's face in her mind's eye. It hadn't mellowed with time. She had been beautiful, possibly more beautiful than Kate. Everybody had said it. She remembered her Uncle Richard at her mother's funeral as he uttered hollow words at her. In truth, Richard couldn't stomach being in the same room as his sister. The relationship had been rotten from a young age, and Kate had imagined that her mother had always been poisonous. Richard was a gentle kind man who Kate longed to have a relationship with. However, she feared that he would look at her with that same fearful mistrust that she saw when he spoke of her mother. His mouth paid lip service to his dead sister, but his eyes mirrored the forty years of dislike and jealousy that had built up the walls that separated them. He had never found forgiveness for Annie Marshall. Neither had Kate. Her mother would remain her biggest demon and one day, her little boy would come to her funeral and he would have the same dislike and mistrust that she and Richard had shared. That ached in her more than any other feeling that she endured. She feared that her longing to be loved by her son would be the end of her. Yet, she knew she couldn't return to him. For as long as Kate would live, and that might not be long if Bruce Anders had his way, her disappointment in herself would burn as brightly as her hatred of her mother.

25.
Phil Morris sat at his laptop and searched the database for every paroled criminal who had been charged with arson in the past three years. He wanted to go farther back in his search but, so far, it had left him with dead end after dead end. Whatever scenario he came up with, he just kept coming back to the same conclusion. It was either an insurance job or payback. Forensics had now presented him with a report. The fire had only escalated onto the top two floors because there had been an assortment of flammable liquids stored within the building. Forensics had found wax paper residue in some of the rooms which would have also helped spread the fire quicker, but the forensic team sense that such items might be there naturally. The accelerant used to start the fire on the ground floor had only been sprayed to the foot of the stairs. Phil found this strangest because the dead body that still remained unidentified, had been upstairs. Why would somebody try to conceal a body by burning it, but not pour the accelerant anywhere near it? It didn't make sense.

He looked at Bruce Anders first of all. No criminal record to speak of, aside from a few drunken brawls at the tail end of his teen years. He was either very clean or very clever, and Phil knew where his betting money lay. So far, there had been no suggestion of money troubles. Bruce had various business interests and seemed to have a healthy enough bank balance. He had just bought that new property on the river side. His motivation, by all accounts, didn't appear to be money. So, if it wasn't money, then surely that eliminated Bruce. This then brought him to the next suspect.

Kate had already accounted for her whereabouts that night. It had already been confirmed with the manager of the bar that she had been drinking in. Right now, he had eliminated her from his enquiries completely. What if she was lying though? What if she had set it up so that she could be somewhere public and create a very public scene? She had threatened Bruce not long before. Was she capable of murder though? Phil didn't think it very likely. Besides, if she had threatened Bruce, why was it not his murder that they were investigating? Mistaken identity? Was it possible that Kate had gone there to confront him and had accidentally killed somebody else? Phil's head was starting to hurt from all the possible scenarios.

Phil's eyes started to glaze over as he realised that he had been staring at the laptop for the last couple of hours. He finally called it a day and saw that it was time to head home for a quick bite. Kate had promised to cook dinner as a thank you for giving her a bed. He felt guilty then for even suspecting her in such a heinous crime. Perhaps he would go back to the scene of the fire. Maybe he had missed something the first time. Maybe forensics had. One thing he was sure of though was that Kate Mulgrew was definitely not guilty of murder or arson. If he really were a betting man, he would put a month's salary on it. Right now, prior to hitting the investigation trail with Donna, he just wanted to get home and taste whatever culinary delights Kate had conjured up for him.

He raced through rush hour traffic with the intent of heading back out for eight p.m. His mobile suddenly flashed up unknown number on the screen. He reached towards the dash board and heard a voice boom to life through the car speaker.

"Hi, Phil. It's Carrie," she sounded impatient and excitable. She had news for him. He could tell it as soon as her voice came cracking into his car.

"Hey, Carrie. Okay, you got something for me?" She paused for a moment and he could almost sense the palpitation on her breath.

"I've got an identity for you. We've finally managed to identify the body that you found in that fire."

26.

Bruce was wiping down the bar and putting away the last of a batch of dirty glasses when DI Phil Morris and Donna Barclay ambled through the door. Bruce groaned loudly and carried on with the task in hand.

"Evening, Mr Anders." Bruce smiled wryly and nudged his head. Phil eyed the empty bar and nodded his appreciation for the place. He had been here before, on several occasions, but he didn't recall ever meeting Bruce. A long plank of dark oak hovered four foot above a reflective glass bar that housed an endless range of the finest whiskey's Phil had seen. The lights had been dimmed, revealing just enough for Bruce to carry out the last of his graft for the night. As the swinging beat of a jazz tune soothed through the air, Phil tapped his finger lightly against his upper thigh. Donna merely looked around the place inquisitively. How did somebody like Bruce, a burling absconder of Glasgow's once notorious schemes, acquire such a place?

"Nice place, I don't think I've ever been," she offered breezily, biting her lower lip. Bruce watched her loom behind Phil Morris as he drew closer. Even at four inches short of Bruce's towering height, he was the very essence of authority. A lesser man might have been intimidated.

"I'm sure you folks don't drink on the job, but I can rustle you up the finest cappuccino this side of the river." Phil thought Bruce seemed more hospitable this time round. That made him suspicious. The nicer people became during an investigation, the more they had to hide.

"I'm fine, thanks Mr Anders. I just have some questions for you?" Donna didn't answer.

"Okay," Bruce sighed again and stepped out from behind the bar. "What can I do for you Detective?" He perched himself on a bar stool and allowed his shoulders to sag a little.

"The first thing I want to ask you about is the body that was found by the river the night before last." Even the words pained him. To take away her humanity and refer to her as 'the body' made him seethe with rage.

"I heard about it, talk of the place. Homeless, wasn't she?" Bruce clasped his hand together and rubbed them furtively. Donna narrowed her eyes. Was he nervous? Was that sweat she could see on his palms?

"Somebody told you that?" Phil moved towards him and rested his hand upon a stool that stood opposite to where Bruce sat.

"Yes. Just about every customer that came in yesterday and today. Although, I'm not sure why you want to speak to me about it? Unless you think that she burned my club down or something," he laughed sarcastically. Phil eyed him angrily. This guy really grated on him. He seemed to suck the light out of everything around him. For that alone, Phil wanted to break him in half.

"I'm not sure that it does have anything to do with you yet." There was an emphatic tone to Phil's answer, and it wasn't lost on either Donna or Bruce. "I should mention though, Mr Anders, that she was sleeping rough with a girl who I believe you know."

"I know a lot of girls." Bruce stared at the Detectives and tugged on the sleeve of his t-shirt. Was he nervous? Confused? Donna thought that he seemed a little shiftier than her previous encounter with him. Did he have something to hide? Was he tired after a long day on his feet?

"This one was on the list of possible grudges that you gave to me."

"Really, that surprises me," Bruce suddenly snapped, an edge creeping into his voice that Phil hadn't experienced before. "I vet my girls very carefully Detective. I don't do alcoholics, junkies or homeless people. Do you think the guys who come for a lap dance at my club are interested in girls who stink of booze, wear injection marks as a fashion accessory or stink of three-day-old body odour?"

"You make a very good point. But I think this girl was new to the street. Perhaps you firing her might have something to do with her having to make herself homeless." Phil spoke slowly now, tension spreading through his tone. The previous song ended on the jukebox and filled the room with an awkward silence before another song that Phil recognised soothed into the air.

"So who was it then?" Bruce asked impatiently, lifting his right hand forcefully.

"Kathryn Mulgrew." Bruce's posture changed instantly, his body becoming so rigid that he almost looked like a mannequin.

"So she burned my club down and... what? Killed that old homeless girl?" Neither Donna nor Phil answered right away. The pause was long enough to enrage Bruce who seemed to develop a tic upon the side of his mouth.

"I don't believe Kathryn Mulgrew burned your club down, and I don't think you believe it either." Bruce stood up from his stool then, his shoulders squaring until he blocked the light from the back side of the bar.

"So, you've not arrested her?" He licked his lip anxiously. Phil pursed his lips and turned to meet Donna's gaze.

"How long did she work for you?" Bruce seemed to think for a moment, trying to peg the exact moment that she had started working for him.

"A few weeks. Not one of my better decisions," he finally replied, and Phil noted the sourness in his answer.

"Why's that?" Outside, drunkards rolled past, clamouring towards the centre of town.

"She was volatile. Argumentative! It was just as I told you the other day, Detective; she was bad for the morale of the other girls." The rally outside quietened then, and only the music from inside the bar defused the tension that wafted around them.

"So she stood up for herself?" It was Donna who spoke now, advocating for women everywhere no doubt.

"She had a bad attitude, detective. I'm sure you appreciate the need for staff to comply with the rules. She wanted a job. I gave her one. She wound everybody up. I had girl who've worked for me for years suddenly coming and bitching about the conditions, about the customers, about the pay."

"Don't you welcome critique from your staff, Mr Anders?" His eyes widened slightly as if he had been caught between the wire. His mind erupted into a state of contradiction.

"Yes, I do. If it's fair. My girls are well treated up at the club, Detective Morris. If they have a problem with an amorous customer, they can come to me. Kate was causing unnecessary upset." Phil nodded his head then.

"So, what you're saying is that the girls should only come to you if they are on the verge of being raped. Otherwise, shut up and put up."

"That's NOT what I said," Bruce bellowed. "Look, why do I feel like the one on trial here. Kate Mulgrew is a crank. She threatened me. She threatened my business. Only days before it burned to the ground. My business is dead. Two people that she has had direct contact with are dead. I don't understand why you haven't arrested her yet." His voice was calmer now, returning him to the measured man that Phil had met on previous occasions. In some way, Phil actually agreed with his reasoning. Everything he said was correct. She had threatened him, the club had burned down, and she did have access to both of the victims. However, they were once again forgetting something.

"She has an alibi, Mr Anders. For both nights. So that theory seems as dead as your lap dancing club." He smiled then, a toothy grin that sent a shudder through Bruce.

"I'll bet my life on her being guilty and that she's got somebody covering for her." He spoke desperately now. Why was he so keen on pinning the blame on Kate Mulgrew? What was he hiding himself?

"I wouldn't play fast and loose with your life Mr Anders. The girl's not guilty," he paused and enjoyed Bruce's silence. "On the subject of the other body, by the way, I do have a few questions. Forensics have just given me a positive identification." Bruce looked up quickly, his stony face tightening. He looked surprised, but he didn't speak. He simply stared at Phil in anticipation. "I know what you're thinking Mr

Anders. Most people think that a body cremated in those kinds of conditions will be unidentifiable, but they'd be wrong."

"You know who she is?" Phil moved away from Bruce and stood casually beside Donna.

"We do, Mr Anders. But it wasn't a 'she'; it was a 'he'."

27.
Two lines of traffic snaked along the snow-capped roads until the Clyde pathway became grid locked. Sirens howled in the distance whilst a tall man in a black cap played an oboe on the next street corner. The man stepped out of the car, ground his shoe into the white slush and grimaced at the slew of Christmas shoppers who had already started to rush buy. He had watched the traffic start and stop with enduring patience, each inconvenienced person mithering in their swollen indifference. His eyes searched for Kate Mulgrew, basking in his own arrogant assertion that she wouldn't have gone far from here. Hours had passed since his arrival, and he had viewed the congregation for the old dead woman from its inception. It was an impressive turn out, he mused, wondering if that many people would care if he were to die. He didn't think so although he knew that death brought the bulging eyes and grasping hands of sweeping vultures.

      As early afternoon approached, it irked him to realise that perhaps Kate wasn't coming at all. He had entered and exited the car, adjusting the heating within, with astounding regularity. The wait was becoming tiring, and his temperament was becoming fractious. His toes stung from the cold now and, as he rested his hands on the metal of his car roof, his reddening fingers were beginning to curl into a frozen curve. He didn't know how much longer he could remain this static. All he did know was that he wanted to get to her so badly that it forced his heart to speed and his blood to pump at a dangerous level. Then, the city became swallowed in white again, as the snow began to fall from the skies. He lowered himself back into the vehicle and banged his fists against the wheel. Where the hell was she? He could see his breath against the numbing air, even inside the warmth of the car, and he checked his reflection in the mirror. Crow's feet deepened within his grimace and he saw the anger blaze in his eyes. He wasn't leaving here without, at the very least, seeing her.

28.

A deepening throng of vagrants were gathering away from the vexatious pry of media eyes. As had been threatened, snow had finally fallen across the towering expanse of the central belt, forming a flat white cap upon its surface. As Kate made her way through the labyrinth of Glasgow, she waved away the drift of snow that landed upon the hood of the jacket she had borrowed from Phil Morris. As soon as she turned onto the Clyde strip, she could see the army of drifters and travellers who had congregated to pay their final respects to Florence. The news of her death had spread like dust in the wind and had been met with a mixture of anger and fear.

Kate thought back to that moment where she had been told of Flo's death. DI Phil Morris had woken Kate gently in the night to deliver the news and, despite their short acquaintanceship, she had sobbed like a child in his arms. She didn't know how she could feel such grief for a person she barely knew when she had struggled to muster a single tear for her own dying mother, but when those tears filled her helpless eyes, they had threatened never to stop. She had fallen onto the bed in Phil's spare room and, unable to drift into the tiniest semblance of unconsciousness, she had recalled the old woman's cackling laugh and her ability to poke enormous fun at those more fortunate than her.

Kate blanched as she tucked herself between Marv and a rather portly woman who oozed an acrid smell of stale alcohol and clothes that had probably never seen the inside of a washing machine. They stood just yards from Flo's patch and huddled over a caricature drawing of Flo that Marv had held in his possession for years.

"She hated that picture, so she did." Kate hadn't realised it until he spoke, but she had never heard his voice before. It was softer and more gentlemanly that she might have imagined. A minority of the mourner's laughed then, and Kate thought that Flo might have appreciated the laughter more than the tears. She wondered then just what the old woman had endured in those final moments of her life. She wasn't sure if Phil had been cautious with the details of her death because they were too disturbing to share, or because he simply didn't have any answers. As she sobbed onto the sleeve of his jacket, she heard various anecdotes about Flo's life from the people who had known her for all of these years.

Since Kate's arrival, the crowd had almost doubled, and a young woman with track marks on her arms began to hum the opening bars of Ben E. King's Stand By Me. Her voice was surprisingly soothing and tuneful as it rolled onto the river and reverberated in the cold. It was a rare graceful moment for a life that had been savagely shortened. As the man beside the singer began to harmonise, other voices joined in until the tune fell away and fused into something less beautiful but, nonetheless, moving. Kate felt ridiculous. Although nobody commented, she had known Flo so little time that she didn't feel that she deserved to be here. She was sharing in the grief of people who had known Flo for a lifetime in comparison. She felt Marv tuck his arm around hers and give her a gentle nudge.

As the young woman belted out a final note, waving her hand emphatically, Kate suddenly noticed a man standing at the side of a pillar beneath the bridge. He wasn't standing with the crowd of mourners, but he watched attentively as they fell into another tune. Kate became so distracted that she stopped mouthing along with the singing. The man seemed to be staring directly at her. His attire, a black suit and white shirt ensemble, looked entirely appropriate for a funeral or wake. Yet, he looked wholly out of place when contrasted with those who clustered together for the purpose of Flo's memorial and the promise of a much needed heat.

As the man continued to stare into the crowd, Kate became quite unnerved. She didn't know if the icy chill she felt was from the growing dread or the falling snow but, as her body froze in place, she suddenly realised that she recognised him. She had seen him at the club. The unease rose in her stomach and orbed into a fear that filled her chest and intensified her breathing. She pulled away from Marv, unlocking her arm from his, and moved towards the suited man. Why was he following her? Had she finally come face to face with the person who had been trailing her throughout the city? She wanted to scream out, but she also wanted to confront him and demand answers. She moved towards him and, as she did, he turned to walk away.

"Hey!" She called out after him but he didn't seem to hear her. She rubbed her hands together because the cold was so piercing that it touched her flesh. He looked back and saw the guilt flush his face. "Hey, I'm talking to you." She trudged through the inch of snow that had now settled on the tarmac and felt it fluff upon her toes. Then, as he began to race towards his car, she raced towards a turret of stairs that would allow her to gain just enough to cut off his path. As she flew up the stairs, her fear giving way to her need to know, she suddenly felt her heel insert itself in the square of an iron grid and hold tightly in place. She screamed again. She then wrestled with her leg and tried to free her shoe from the grid. Short of breaking the heel, she knew the only other way to catch up with him before he fled was to release her foot from the shoe. It was the only pair she owned.

She could still see him move quickly across to the other side of the street where he had evidently parked the car. She quickly reached down and unstrapped her foot from the inside of the shoe and left it wielded there. She felt the freeze of the snow nip at the arch of her foot as she made her way out onto the main strip. She was aware that the singing had stopped now and that the crowd were moving towards her. She stood on the pavement and saw the man fumble with his key and race into his car. She gasped. Why had he been following her? She had exchanged some pleasantries with him at the club, but she had never actually had sex with him. She felt the alarm jet through her again and watched helplessly as Peter Dow drove until he simply vanished.

29.

From inside the fog Mrs Petrie saw a man and a woman emerge. They had parked their car on the other side of the road and made their way towards her front door. She peeked through the curtains and waited for them to climb the stairs and ring her door bell. The green door creaked open and revealed the two police officers and their out held badges. She recognised Phil Morris immediately from his previous visit to the burned down club. A week had passed since then.

"DI Morris and Harvey, Mrs Petrie. Do you have a few minutes?" Mrs Petrie was a small frail woman with an arch in her back that made her appear smaller than she probably was. Her grey hair was thin and weedy and framed caramel coloured eyes upon a portly face that looked misshapen upon her bony body. Her skin was naturally pale and led to a set of thin lips the colour of a fading rose.

"I really don't know how much help I can be to you both. I generally mind my own business." She spoke swiftly as she ushered them into a large dark lounge that adorned more photos of children than Phil had ever seen.

"Your grandchildren?" He nodded towards the variance of photos admirably and seemed to hit just the right nerve because her thin rose coloured lips twisted into an immodest smile that barely contained beaming pride.

"I have fourteen and a new great grandchild. They're a prize Detective. Do you have children of your own?" Phil merely shook his head, and the old woman searched his face for an inflection of sadness. She found none.

"I have twins, a year old," Donna was quick to boast her own little bundles of joy, although she hadn't been calling them anything remotely close to joyful at six that morning when they had screamed merry murder from the top of her house to the bottom. Ashen eyed and devoid of sleep, she now feigned a proud smile and joined the ranks of those women who daren't ever say that motherhood was a toil. She sensed that Mrs Petrie's smile was just as insincere. For all the pictures that hanged from her wall, there wasn't a sense that a child had ever been present in this house.

"Tea or coffee?" Phil had been offered more tea and coffee this week than he knew it was possible to drink. Truth be known, he longed for the sandy beaches of foreign lands where he could sip on a large cocktail instead.

"No, thanks Mrs Petrie. I'm off caffeine for the foreseeable."

"I wish I was, I'm kept awake half the night because I drink too much of it," she tutted to herself, and indicated for them to take a seat.

"You should consider decaf. Best thing I ever did," Donna offered half-heartedly and then sat at the end of the sofa beside Phil.

"I'll think about that. Thank you. Now, how can I help you?" She looked impatient now and Donna realised they had maybe outstretched the pleasantries.

"Firstly, I just want to ask if you saw anything out of the ordinary on the night of the fire?" It was Phil who spoke now and as he did, he eyed the window and the gap between the curtains and it didn't shock him to realise that Mrs Petrie was somebody who probably spent an inordinate amount of time peering through those curtains, just as she had been when he and Donna had arrived.

"Let me think. Was that the Saturday night? I came home from prayer meeting at around seven o'clock. I then had the television on in the background. I don't really recall what I was doing in between. I think I watered the plants, had a bowl of soup and then maybe sorted through my mail. Then all of a sudden, the ten o'clock news came on and I remember wondering where the hours had gone." Her voice lifted slightly and Phil found humour in the dramatic way in which she described her not very eventful evening.

"So, at that point, there was nothing that drew your attention to the club?" he asked solemnly, masking his underlying amusement.

"Well, the club was closed unusually early, I know that. Sometimes those girls were coming and going at all hours, but it was in complete darkness before eleven o'clock." Phil had already thought it strange that the club closed so early.

Most lap dancing clubs that he knew of operated well into the night. It seemed bewildering to him that this particular club operated in daytime hours and that it operated in an area that might be deemed too respectable for such an establishment to exist.

"And that wasn't normal?" Donna watched as Mrs Petrie fluffed a cushion and mulled over her question.

"It happened, but rarely," she opined as she rested onto the back rest of the chair. She eyed Detective Morris as he scribbled onto his little notepad. She wondered how much he would get onto that little page before he'd have to turn onto the next one. He seemed to be writing for the longest time. As a shorthand expert, Mrs Petrie found it infuriating to watch somebody scribble lengthy notes. Then he looked up again, and she found herself gazing admiringly at his face. He was a man who she imagined had been handsome when he was young, but who now bore the traits of a refined gentleman. She also felt an affinity with the kindness that spread through his eyes.

"But there was nothing else unusual?" Phil Morris spoke again, this time more persistent, pushing her towards some sort of resolve.

"Well…" she paused then, as if she were reliving the memory. "I saw the last of the girl's coming out round about that time. And I saw Bill Walker from the next house walking his dog."

"From number 18?" She flinched then, as if she had handed his name over too freely.

"Yes. He was later than usual. That was strange as he normally walked Bosco much earlier." Mrs Petrie stuttered, fearing she might have said too much. There wasn't a crime in changing the time that you walked your dog, though, so she relaxed her poise and smiled gently.

"So, at what time did you realise that the club was on fire?" That was the crux of it; the reason they were all here. To establish exactly what had happened to David King prior to fire ripping through the entire building. Mrs Petrie looked pensively at her clock and then turned back to meet the gaze of the Detective's. She looked embarrassed.

"Well, I didn't realise it was on fire until I heard the sirens." She sounded apologetic as if missing the fire was a reflection on her as a person.

"Okay, Mrs Petrie, thank you," Donna said genuinely and took the woman's tiny hand in hers. Phil Morris stood and moved towards the lounge door, winking gently at Mrs Petrie and enjoying the little flush across her elderly face.

"I'm sorry; I haven't been more help officer." Phil turned towards her and smiled.

"You've been more helpful than you know." He had meant it. She had told him nothing of genuine value, but she had put a tiny slant of perspective on the events leading to the discovery of the fire. He knew now that the fire itself hadn't killed David King. He had been dead long before the fire had even reached that room. Therefore, he had surmised that the fire had been designed to cover up the murder, to throw him off the scent. Then, he thought of something else. He reached into his pocket and pulled out a photograph. He held it towards Mrs Petrie.

"One more thing, Mrs Petrie, do you recognise this man?" She studied the photo intensely. The man in it was younger than Phil. He wore a cocky grin, his hair was dishevelled, and a blue denim jacket matched the colour of his eyes. It was a picture of David King. Mrs Petrie said that she never seen him before, and nothing in her face suggested that she was lying.

"By the way officer, you might want to speak to the Walkers. They have also had some trouble. Whoever set that fire is probably the same person who set their hut on fire." Phil and Donna both looked surprised. They had heard nothing about another fire. Surely, after such a major crime had taken place, anything vaguely linked would be passed to them. Phil felt irritation then.

"They had a fire?"

"Yes!" Mrs Petrie looked vague, like she was trying to find a memory that was stored away. She clasped her hands together and moved to escort them to the door.

"When?" Phil prevented her from moving any further, sure then that she might know more than she was saying.

"The day after, I think." She had passed the knowledge flippantly, but now she realised that she had perhaps said too much. She hoped she hadn't caused trouble for the Walkers. They were going through enough at the moment. She wanted to reach out for the words that had rolled from her tongue, grab them all, and force them back in. However, what was said could not be unsaid. So she just hoped that they weren't too angry with her.

"And that would be in their back garden?" Phil could sense her apprehension. It was written all over her face. There had been nothing particularly suspicious in anything that she said. The only new information was about the fire in their hut. He had assumed that the information had not been passed to him by a colleague, but now he suspected that it just hadn't been reported.

"Yes. They've got a massive garden. Not like my pokey hole." She laughed then, nervously, and escorted them to the front door. They thanked her for her time and stepped back into the fog. They could only just see the top of the burned out building on the peak of the city centre.

"You don't think that the Walkers fire would have been set by the same person, do you?" The thought hadn't left his mind since Mrs Petrie's strange revelation. Whoever had set the fire had done so to conceal the dead body. What possible motive could they have for coming back a day later to set fire to a hut? Was it a warning to the Walkers? Had they seen something?

"I don't know Donna, but if the Walkers know something and they're too afraid to speak, then I think they might be in danger. I think it's time for us to have a conversation with them ourselves."

30.
Three days had passed since Kate's humiliating skirmish with the man in the black suit. Why had Peter Dow been following her and what possible motivation could he have? She wasn't sure about the car because she had only ever seen it at night and it didn't look as dark in the daytime. Why did she have more questions than answers? Who had killed Flo? Did it have something to do with her?

As he had left for work this morning, Phil had left her with a name to search. It was confidential and he shouldn't have been giving her it, he warned. It might help explain exactly who the old woman was though. So, she had taken the dog for a walk in the nearby park which also helped to blow the cobwebs out of her mind. She needed answers. She didn't know why, but she felt that if she knew more about Flo that it might be the key to unlocking her own puzzle.

She slumped into a chair in his tiny office, a room as glum as every other in his bachelor pad. She turned slowly and powered up his laptop. She moved the brown envelope at the side of the laptop further to the side so that she could move the mouse and navigate into the search engine. She felt anxious as it fired to life. Why didn't he have a password, she wondered? For a police officer, he was a little easy on security, she realised. She smiled when she thought about him though. She spun a little on the chair, kicking her feet excitedly. Who was this man who had brought her into his house and saved her from the clutches of the cold grey city?

Finally, when the search engine blazoned across the laptop screen, she typed in the old woman's real name. 'Jessica Dow'. Then, as she typed it, she felt utterly foolish for not making the connection earlier. Dow? Peter hadn't been at Flo's wake because he was following Kate, he had been there because they must have been related. There were several thousand results for her to choose from. She added 'Glasgow' to her search, which appeared to reduce the search results tenfold. Finally, she came across an article that looked vaguely interesting. She clicked slowly and waited on the article to load. A photograph began to appear of a woman much younger than Flo; a respectable wealthy looking woman who had been beautiful and happy looking. There was no mistaking the eyes though. Flo had been Jessica Dow for the first years of her life. What had happened that had taken her to the streets? Kate read the article aloud and gasped.

"Mrs Dow, wife of affluent banker Alexander Dow, mother of Peter, was involved in a crash that killed a 23-year-old father of two. Mrs Dow was unavailable for comment at the time of print, but is said to have sustained minor injuries." Kate looked at the photo again. Jessica really had been quite stunning. Not beautiful in the way that Kate was, but elegant and well groomed, and the sort of woman who married rich affluent men. Kate had known that just from speaking with her. She felt a sadness then, for all the years that Flo must have lost. She clicked on the back arrow and changed the search to 'Jessica Dow accident Glasgow.'

A smaller selection of links flashed up then, and Kate found something even more informative than the previous article. It featured a picture of an elderly man; Alexander Dow, and a teenager who was undoubtedly the young Peter Dow. The article itself spoke about their desperation to find Jessica who had disappeared after the accident. She had sunk into despair and guilt after the death of the young man. However, the article revealed, the third driver involved in the accident had tested positive for a high consumption of alcohol and had been responsible for causing the crash. She could come home now, they said, because she had nothing to feel guilty for. Even the young man's widow had commented, begging Jessica to come home to her family.

Kate read through the remaining article and wept as she viewed the picture of Jessica once again. She had been so consumed by guilt that she had left her own family in the belief that she had destroyed somebody else's family. Had she ever learned the truth, Kate wondered? To live all those years with guilt and to die having never learned the truth sent an ache surging through Kate's body and she longed to tell the old woman that she could go home now. It was too late though. She wondered then how long Peter Dow had known of his mother's whereabouts and had he tried to convince her to go home? What that family must have endured since that terrible rainy night where Josh Divers had been killed was simply unthinkable.

Kate closed the internet page and gasped. She felt as if all of her emotions had been tangled up and wrung out, and she had no more tears left. She fell back into the chair and stared at the blue desktop for twenty minutes. Flo, the kind old woman with the wicked cackle, had been somebody important in Glasgow. Then, with barely a bye or leave, she had become somebody who didn't matter anymore. Kate felt guilty then because she had left her own life for reasons that now seemed trivial and vain. She had walked out, not to protect her family from a shameful secret, but because she was selfish and weak. Suddenly, an icon on the desktop caught her eye and pulled her from the mire of self-pity that she was about to enter into. It was a video file that simply had 'Flo' as its title. As she considered opening the file, she looked back to ensure that Phil hadn't come home and slipped in quietly. If she felt this guilty, then she knew she shouldn't be looking. However, curiosity tugged at her and she finally clicked on the icon twice in quick succession.

The video was grainy, but she could see two figures locked in some kind of embrace. The video was taken from a downward angle, and Kate realised that it was the bridge that she had spent those nights sleeping under. She inhaled a breath of horror then as she realised exactly what she was looking at. It wasn't an embrace that she was viewing. It was Flo's murder. Somebody had filmed it and sent it to Phil Morris. What kind of sick perverted mind did that? Her eyes were agape in revulsion as the video came to a close and faded to a black screen. She hadn't seen the face of the person who had committed the murder as it had been too small. She felt the urge to watch again and see if she could zoom in, but she wasn't computer savvy enough to navigate her way round the laptop. She heaved her chest then, frustrated and defeated. Then, she saw the envelope on the side of the laptop and noticed that it also had the word 'Flo' on it. She ripped it open without regard for being caught and snatched a series of photographs from inside. They were grainy stills from the video. They had been zoomed in on, but there was no mistaking the face of the person who had plunged the knife into Flo's stomach. Staring back at her from the glossy black and white print was the pixilated face of Jennifer Dixon.

31.

"I'm sorry about the smell of petrol." Phil Morris couldn't smell any petrol as he walked into the Walker household. In fact, it was the aroma of bleach that crept up his nostrils and burned at the tiny hairs.

"Elena, let the Detectives in." Bill Walker appeared in the doorway of the lounge. In every way, their house was similar to Mrs Petrie's except for the décor. Theirs was brighter, modern, not as cluttered or as clumsy. "Come through, I've been expecting you." Had Mrs Petrie phoned ahead and warned him that they were on their way.

"Sorry to trouble you. We haven't met yet. This is Detective Donna Barclay and I'm DI Phil Morris. I know you've given a statement to one of our officer's, but there are just a few things I want to clarify."

"No problem, I'm Bill Walker, and this is my wife Elena. Please sit." He held his hand towards the other sofa indicating where he would like them to sit. Elena Walker sat beside her husband, but hid behind him so that she had to peer round him if she wanted to speak. She twitched nervously, rubbing the tips of her fingers together nervously. Suddenly, by way of welcome distraction, Phil's mobile ringtone came to life. He quickly apologised and reached for the off button.

"I hear you had a fire the day after the club next door burned down? Did you report that?" Bill put his hand on his wife's leg.

"No, we didn't," his eyes blinked repeatedly, a nervous tic that made Phil wonder if he had something to hide, "I didn't think it necessary. You fellows have enough to do out catching real criminals." Phil didn't accept his explanation at all. If he could go back through the reasons he had been given for not reporting crimes, 'We didn't want to waste police time' usually equated with 'I'm hiding something', which only confirmed Phi's existing suspicions. Phil was determined to find out what.

"Did it occur to you that the perpetrator of the second fire might have been the person responsible for the first one?" Bill blinked nervously again. He was a broad man with silver hair brushed into a side parting and an air of arrogance that made him look superior and pompous. He was quite a contrast with his striking wife who was remarkably attractive for somebody probably in her late sixties, but who had a permanently distant look in her eyes and seemed to disengage and then re-engage with them on will.

"Yes," he snapped, "Of course it occurred to me. They set fire to our summer house, burned it to the bloody ground." His cheeks filled with air as he blustered, leaving him to exhale loudly when he had finally finished. His face had flushed a little.

"It left a dreadful smell of petrol." It was Elena who spoke again now, repeating what appeared to be her mantra. Phil could only guess that she had become obsessed with the scent and had gone to town with a bottle of bleach because she had eradicated any smell of petrol that she spoke of. Her husband smiled impatiently.

"Yes, that's fine Elena. Anyway Detective, would you care to carry on?" With his wife dutifully put back in her place, Phil nodded.

"Did you see anything suspicious yourself on the evening in question?"

"Well, I was out walking the dog at around eight-ish. It was the usual comings and goings at that time. Men in business suits going in, girls in virtually nothing coming out. I'm sure you're informed as to what type of venue it is, Detective." He looked perturbed as he spoke, resting both hands on his bulging stomach.

"What about you Mrs Walker?" Donna entered into the conversation now. Elena Walker's anxiety wasn't lost on her, and she wanted to know why. Bill seemed to quash her so that she sat in the background and said very little. Donna wasn't sure why, but she would bet her life that it was because she saw something and he had insisted that they shouldn't get involved. That could be why they didn't report the fire in their own back garden.

"No, I didn't leave the house all night, but the next day, the smell of petrol was terrible. I had to scrub the floors and the walls to get rid of the smell." Mrs Walker answered concisely with her previous answers, but continued to add nothing more to proceedings. Phil was becoming frustrated. He would like to speak to them both alone. He might get more answers that way as, together, they seemed to lock down.

"Mrs Walker, would it be any trouble if I asked for some water?" She looked at her husband who simply nodded. "Detective, what about you?" Phil narrowed his eyes indicatively, and she picked up on his signal immediately.

"Some water's fine for me too." Mrs Walker scurried out of the lounge and headed for the kitchen. Moments later, they could hear the clattering of glasses and the gushing of water through the pipes.

"Detective, if I can just put you in the picture. My wife was diagnosed with Alzheimer's ten years ago." Bill Walker waited to his wife was completely out of earshot before he explained her vacant and erratic behaviour. It certainly explained the glazed look in her eyes and her lack of commitment to any conversation.

"I'm sorry."

"No, not at all. She has more good days than bad. It hasn't completely derailed her yet, but she does get repetitive and she focuses on certain things. She has also found this whole affair very upsetting, so I'd prefer that she wasn't involved." It explained why they hadn't wanted to get involved after their own summer house had been burned down. Mrs Walker was probably so distressed by the whole affair that her husband had weighed up the cost to themselves against their investigation.

"If we can avoid upsetting your wife, Mr Walker, you have my word that we will avoid it. However, if she knows anything that helps us find the killer, then we would have to speak to her." Phil spoke gently, but there was a firmness in his voice that left Mr Walker in no doubt of his message.

"I appreciate that, and I'll help in any way I can, but just leave Elena out of it." He was pleading now. For the first time, Phil was sympathetic towards him. He was an awkward stuffy man, but his intentions towards his wife were admirable. He wanted to protect her at any cost, even if it meant not getting justice for the extreme damage that had been caused to his property.

"We will if we can." Mrs Walker returned to the lounge with a tray gripped in her trembling hands. The glasses clattered, and the water splashed wildly as she set it down on a table. Phil turned his attentions towards Mr Walker again.

"So you didn't notice anything unusual when you were walking your dog. What time did you say that was again?" Phil hadn't realised it at first, but Mr Walker had told him a time that didn't correlate with what Mrs Petrie had said.

"About eight." He repeated the time again. Phil looked at Donna who had also realised that the times didn't match. Had Mrs Petrie been confused?

"No dear, it was later. We watched that show that you like, what's it called…?" A moment of clarity from Mrs Walker then, who was contradicting her husband. He flinched momentarily and reached for a glass of water.

"Oh of course, so it was. So it might have been about eleven instead," he concluded matter-of-factly.

"There's a big difference between eight and eleven, Mr Walker. I can understand you being confused by ten minutes or half an hour, but three hours is a long time to be out." Phil eyed the older gentleman without expression, awaiting his response. Bill Walker simply shrugged.

"And that's when I started to smell the petrol, wasn't it dear?" Elena shuddered then, as if she were smelling it and reliving it all over again.

"No, that was the next day, when we discovered the summer house on fire." Bill corrected her, a sliver of annoyance creeping into his steady voice.

"Oh yes. You're right, of course," she looked vacant again. He had muddied her thoughts, and her clarity had disappeared as quickly as it had appeared. Phil watched the interaction between the two of them. He was certainly controlling. Had he always been this way, he wondered? Or was it something that had come as Mrs Walker's condition had deteriorated? She seemed to understand what was going on around her, yet she was so focused on one element of it that he wasn't sure exactly how her answers fitted in with his investigation. He was keen to know what Donna Barclay thought.

"Oh, there was one thing, Detective." He looked at Phil ominously and then reached for his mobile phone. Phil looked up to meet his eyes.

"Something you saw on the night of the fire?"

"No, it was a few days before. I don't even know if it's relevant. They had a regular visit from somebody you might recognise." Phil and Donna looked curious now. Somebody Phil might recognise?

"How so?"

"He's a bit of a local celebrity. An MSP in fact." He winced knowingly then, seemingly pleased that he had offered such a juicy piece of gossip. He handed Phil his mobile phone.

"That's Peter Dow," Donna broke in then, although Phil didn't completely recognise him from the photo on Mr Walker's phone.

"Why did you take this photo, Mr Walker?" Phil asked suspiciously. He watched Mr Walker struggle to find the words to justify the photo as his face became redder.

"We don't often get famous faces round here. Especially in a place of distasteful repute. So I wanted to show it around. You know, just for laughs." Phil cringed.

"A man's reputation is not for laughs, Mr Walker." He sounded angry now.

"Then he shouldn't have gone there." Wasn't that the truth? Peter Dow had put himself in the firing line by attending a whorehouse. Phil was joining the dots now. It wasn't only Kate that had linked the club to Flo. Peter Dow shared the same surname and Phil was willing to bet that an internet search would show that they were related in some way. He quickly forwarded the photo to his own mobile number as Mr Walker fussed over the glasses of water.

Phil switched his mobile phone back on as he reached the bottom of the stairs outside the Walker household. An MMS message flashed up with the photo of Peter Dow.

"What did you make of them, Phil?" Donna had read his mind, again. It was why he loved working with her. She got him completely. They finished each other's sentences. They saw most things from the same perspective and when they didn't, it was usually because they were both wrong.

"He's hiding something. I don't know if it's just to protect his wife or if they know something that they don't want to tell us." He saw that he had a missed call from his home number. Kate had tried to call him. He hadn't yet told Donna that he had the girl living with him for the past week. He could hear the judgement drip from her voice before she'd even spoken, so he'd opted not to mention it. He would check in with her shortly but, for now, he had more pressing things to take care of.

32.
As she waited impatiently for Phil to call her back, Kate fiddled with the buttons on the phone and sighed loudly. As she fiddled with the soft caramel fur on the back of the dog, he gave her a look of disgust. Even the dog had become tired of her, she thought to herself, as she journeyed through an endless stream of confusing feelings. Jennifer Dixon has murdered Flo? Why? It didn't make any sense. They had only met for a few seconds. She couldn't take her eyes of the picture, the sickening image of a killer staring back at her. She could snap Jennifer's neck in two if she could get close enough to her.

Musky suddenly started barking, startling Kate so that she almost dropped the glass of water that she held in her hand. She hadn't heard him really bark quite so ferociously before. She heard the clink of the metal letter box as Musky bound towards the door. Kate placed the glass on the table and followed him into the hallway and watched as a piece of paper finally escaped the letter box and wafted towards the floor. Musky bounced, his front legs lifting him slightly from the ground before he flattened himself out and stretched. His bark lowered to an incessant whine. Thinking it must be a note from a neighbour, Kate unfolded the piece of paper. Suddenly, she felt the urge to scream as she glowered for untold seconds at the writing. Staring back at her were the words, written in red block letters;

KATE, YOU CAN'T START A FIRE IN THE RAIN.

She raced past the dog and ran towards the lounge window. Snow drifted lightly past her eyes. The shackles of panic gripped her tightly as she pushed her hands towards the glass and strained to see through the flakes and the dropping haze. She was too late, for she saw the door of the car that had been following her slam shut. She had been so damn close to seeing who it was that she could almost kick herself. If only she had acted a moment quicker, instead of staring at the words and trying to work out what they meant, she would have been able to identify her stalker. She looked at the whitening sky, dipping into a rising fog, and felt as cold as the air. The world had never looked more dismal to her, and she didn't know whether to cry again or lay down and die. As fear engulfed her, she wasn't sure she had the energy to do either. If she had believed in God, she might have prayed that he give her a fucking break, but she didn't. So, she simply stared into the street where the car of her stalker stubbornly sat.

She moved back from the window in the hope that whoever it was would drive away. She held the note tightly in her hand, fearing that if she let it go, she might just go mad. She had taken comfort when she had realised that it wasn't Peter Dow and that he had his own reasons for being by the river that day. The relief had been short lived. For Kate, knowing who it was couldn't be worse than not knowing at all. She longed for Phil to call her back. Should she call him again? Standing almost a meter from the window, she continued to stare at the car, fearing that if she looked away, she wouldn't see them coming. More than anything, she feared that they'd break Phil's door down before she'd even get a chance to scream for help. So, she stood perfectly still; waiting, breathing, wanting to scream...

33.
The burling scent of alcohol drifted into the air as Peter Dow fell onto his sofa. The room was spinning so quickly that he could no longer keep his balance. His legs felt weak, his hands tingled and his brain seemed unable to connect to the rest of his flailing body. His lounge looked like it hadn't been cleaned in a week. This had been his toughest time. Firstly, he had learned that Dave King had been the dead body in the fire. The news had been delivered by Bruce who seemed to derive pleasure from telling him. Peter had suspected that Bruce had known all along who the victim had been and exactly why he had been there. Worse than this though, his mother had been murdered. He had only recently discovered where she was although he had been too afraid to actually confront her. He wasn't sure if he was more afraid of her rejecting him, or him rejecting her. He didn't have the energy, nor the sobriety, to be angry though. He hadn't had his mother since he was in his teen years, so the woman he had seen by the river was a virtual stranger to him. Still, he had hoped that he would have worked up the courage to introduce himself and perhaps build a relationship with her. What could have been worse than her rejection of him the first time?

Peter had accepted that he was an alcoholic now. It was the one way that he could eliminate the resurgent pain that he felt. Where he had once had a healthy appetite, he now replaced his meals with a variety of drinks. At first, he would tipple just enough to make the day manageable. These past weeks had seen things go from bad to worse. He had been on a binge since the service by the river. Now, his floor was sprinkled with empty spirit bottles and the broken glass of a wine bottle. He had found himself in frequent fits of despair over the days and had cried often for the regret of not rescuing his estranged mother from a life of desperation on the streets. He wanted to shout joyously to her that she had not committed any crime, that it had not been her fault, but her recrimination must have been so deeply burned into her that she might not accept it. He detested himself all over again for not being stronger and not going to her. He could have saved her life.

Bruce Anders let himself in when he found Peter Dow's flat door unlocked. He had been trying to call Peter all day, but the phone had continuously gone to voicemail. He was feeling the pressure from his investors who wanted the casino deal finalised. Bruce couldn't do anything without permission from the local council. He was depending on Peter to push that through, but had learned that the man hadn't even been to his office since the day of his press conference. It didn't shock him to find Peter slumped onto his sofa, anaesthetized by a variance of alcohol. The man looked dreadful, much worse than he had looked a few nights before when they had met. Of course, Bruce had known all along who the woman by the river was. He made it his business to know everybody else's. He had timed the revelation beautifully when he had needed a favour from Peter months before.

"Not a pretty sight, eh Peter?" Peter looked up and crossed his eyes. He could see two of Bruce leaning towards him and, as drunk as he was, he could see the aggression on the bigger man's face. Bruce wasn't here to show concern, or even the slightest humanity for Peter's loss. Instead, he was here to settle a business matter that Peter had failed to deliver on.

"I don't have your permit." His words were slurred and fell into the air like a single syllable. Bruce felt his anger churn, but knew he wouldn't get anywhere with Peter in this state. He went to Peter's kitchen which was no tidier than his lounge and pulled a dirty mug from the sink. After boiling the kettle, and heaping four teaspoons of coffee into the mug, he delivered the drink to Peter. It was strong enough to offset the taste of alcohol in his mouth, but not strong enough to cancel days of persistent drinking. It might just sober him up enough to give Bruce what he wanted. Bruce stared out of the window and across the city whilst Peter drank the coffee, seemingly untroubled by the temperature of the liquid. When it seemed that he was alert enough to understand, Bruce spoke again. This time his voice was lowered into a threatening growl.

"You don't have anybody left Pete, and I know that you don't care very much right now. Even if you don't know it, things can actually get worse than they are right now." He paused emphatically. "I'm sure you'll agree that there's been enough death. It'd be terrible if anybody else were to be hurt." Bruce knew he was clutching at straws. He couldn't think of anybody else who Peter held dearly. Yet, there must be somebody. Nobody could be that pathetic and alone, he thought, unsympathetically. "So, if you want to avoid anymore, get me that fucking permit."

34.

Kate was still hovering behind the curtain and looking at the car on the street when the phone sprung to life. The sharp scream of the ringtone made her jump so quickly that her heart didn't follow right away. She looked back through the window and strained her eyes to see if she could make out a face or an item of clothing or anything that would distinguish whoever sat at the driver's seat. However, shadows crossed the car windows and darkened it so much that she couldn't determine if it was even a man or a woman. She stepped back, still clutching the note, and reached for the phone.

"Hi, it's me; sorry it took me so long to phone back. What a hell of a day I've had." Phil could hear the panic in her breathing before she even uttered a word. "You okay, what's wrong?" His voice rose to mirror her panic.

"The person that's been following me. They're outside. They've posted a note through the door." Her voice was audibly rising. Phil felt helpless at the other side of the city.

"A note? What does it say? Can you see who they are?"

"No, the windows are too dark to make anything out. I don't know what this note means. It could mean anything." She read the words out to him, and it only made his belief stronger that Bruce Anders meant her harm. The reference to 'fire' was enough to cement it for him. Although, he hadn't taken Anders for a stupid man.

"Okay, I want you to remain calm and go next door and chap on Mr Beaton. Do it quickly and pass the phone to him. I'll explain who you are." Kate moved quickly as Phil continued to speak. She unlocked the door slowly and winced as she imagined the person coming back up the stair. Maybe Mr Beaton wouldn't get to the door quickly enough.

"Phil, I'm scared." He wanted so badly to comfort her. To beat the crap out of whoever was doing this to her and to make her know that everything would be okay. The door was slightly ajar now, and she could almost see onto the landing. Then, realising that she might not get another moment like this, she threw open the door and stepped out. She grabbed the railing and shifted towards Mr Beaton's door. She was about to bang loudly on it when she looked out of the landing window and saw the car screech away from the front. They were gone. Leaving a trail of sludge and a terrified woman in their wake. She stepped back again.

"They're gone." She grasped for breath for a moment. "That's not what I phoned you for Phil. I know who the killer is. I saw the video and your prints and I know exactly who she is." She spoke quickly now. Phil felt relief surge through him. He had been waiting on somebody calling him back with a list of names. This made it a whole lot easier. "Jennifer Dixon, Phil. She used to work with me at the club. I have her phone number. Can you trace where she lives. Also, did you know that Flo was Peter Dow's mother"? She sounded excited, and it was a far cry from the panicked woman who had been on the phone a few moments before. She locked his front door again.

"I suspected that. When you told me you thought he was following you, which just didn't make sense. Other than some weird obsession he might have with you, what possible reason could he have for stalking you? Then when I found out Flo's real name, it made absolute sense that they were related. I thought you were the key to linking both killings, but now I'm not so sure. Now I think Peter Dow is the missing link that I've been looking for. Which means…."

"Which means that Jennifer probably burned the club down. That bitch. She was hoping that I would get the blame." Kate was even more furious now. She didn't just want to snap Jennifer's neck, she wanted to dance on her cold dead body, and she loathed herself for having such dark gruesome thoughts. She had only come close to feeling this contempt for one other woman in her entire life. Her mother. Jennifer was worse though. At least her mother hadn't pretended to like her. Jennifer had offered the hand of friendship, but had been plotting behind her back the entire time.

"I do have another theory about the fire at the club. I can't say yet Kate, but do me a favour, stay indoors. If somebody's got it in for you, then you could be next, and I don't want you dead on my watch. Oh and can you give me the number for Jennifer Dixon?"

After reading out the mobile number that Jennifer had given her, she slammed the phone back onto the base and then made her way to the kitchen. She pulled the biggest knife from the drawer that she could find. If somebody was coming for her, she wasn't going down without a fight.

35.

Peter was moderately more clear-headed by the time DI Morris and Barclay arrived at his flat. When they had buzzed in, it gave him just enough time to gather up the broken glass and strewn bottles and lumber them into a plastic bag. He opened a window and sucked in a lungful of air. Then they arrived at the front door and banged loudly. Why did the police always do that, even when you were expecting them? His head hurt, he realised, and he hoped that his hangover wouldn't last as long as his latest dalliance with the bottle. He perched himself back on the sofa as the Detectives entered the lounge.

Of all the homes he had visited during this investigation, Phil admired Peter's the most. It was a new tower block in the city centre of Glasgow which had been squared off to make every flat a different shape. A small veranda veered off from the side of the lounge and faced away from town so that Peter probably got the best of the summer sun when it finally arrived. What wasn't so impressive to him though was that Peter Dow was quite evidently drunk and unable to balance on foot. The stench of stale alcohol was so repugnant that he could feel it tingle at the back of his throat. Donna simply wafted her hand in front of her face and cringed.

"Mr Dow, I'm sorry to hear about your mother. We would have been here sooner had we realised your relationship. Unfortunately, our team were only able to identify her from her DNA yesterday." His eyes drooped and Phil saw him muster them open with all his might.

"Relationship?" Peter let out a cynical laugh. "What relationship? She ran away from us years ago. To me, my mother's been dead for years." He sounded bitter, but Phil sensed that there was more longing hidden away under Peter's sour retort than he would care to admit.

"How long had you known where your mother was?" It was Donna who spoke now, startling Peter who seemed not to notice that she was even present.

"Who said I did?" He was teasing her, because a sardonic smile spread across his face. There was something very guarded about how he spoke though, and Phil sensed that this was a man who had pent up a lifetime of emotional loss and could unravel at any minute. Certainly the odour of fusty booze and his scruffy appearance did nothing to contradict the suggestion.

"You were seen at a small gathering that your mother's friends had for her by the river." Peter looked surprised again. Who had seen him? Who had even known who he was? Then, without really thinking about, he connected the dots together. He knew he had recognised that girl, but it had taken him until now to realise exactly who she was. Kate Mulgrew. He threw his head back and rolled his eyes.

"Mr Dow, did you know a man by the name of David King?" The change of questioning made him quite unsteady. He felt the room shift slightly. He had been thinking about Kate and his mother and the way his mother had died. Suddenly, he found himself trying to think about David King, but his mind was struggling to register all the different people that he was being asked about. Suddenly, he wished he hadn't spent three days throwing drinks down his throat until he had been drawn into this stupor.

"David? Dave? Yes, yeah, I knew Dave. Why?"

"I assume you know about the body at HEELS?" Phil saw him puff his chest out in an attempt to compose himself.

"Where?"

"Mr Dow, we know you were a regular visitor to HEELS. We have various eye witnesses who could place you there, and I have a photo of you leaving there a few days before the place was burned to the ground."

"I had nothing to do with that bloody fire." Peter's voice rose slightly and Phil could see that he was becoming flustered and fretful.

"I know that Mr Dow. Although, I am curious about your relationship with the owner there," Phil pulled his mobile phone from his pocket and flicked open the MMS that he had sent himself from Mr Walker's mobile phone, "as the picture I have is of you leaving his club with him. I'm also curious how somebody who I know worked for you several times over the years ended up stabbed to death in a place that was burned to the ground?" Peter's brain was struggling to digest the information that was being presented to him.

"Detective, I don't know what you're talking about. You're telling me that Dave King is dead?" There was something unnatural about the way he spoke which made both Phil and Donna suspect that he already knew.

"That's exactly what I'm saying, Mr Dow. Do you know a girl by the name of Jennifer Dixon?" Peter had to think for a second. The name didn't instantly strike a chord with him.

"I know a Jennifer. Why?"

"Is this her?" Phil pulled out a small copy of the photo that he had asked somebody to take from the video of her killing Flo. Donna thought it insensitive that Phil should be showing that particular photo to Peter, however she knew it wouldn't be obvious to him where the photo was actually pulled from. So she remained tight-lipped.

"It looks like her, but I can't tell because she's got her hood up and I usually see her with her hair out and her make up on. I would say it was her though." Peter was becoming more sober as the minutes passed. He reached for the half-empty mug of cold coffee that Bruce Anders had left for him and sipped from the rim. Phil watched him intently.

"Mr Dow, we have reason to believe that Jennifer Dixon killed both David King and Jessica Dow, your mother! We also believe that she wasn't acting alone, and that somebody was either paying her or forcing her to do it. We know that she was a prostitute, and that she worked for Bruce Anders. We've also been told that she recently acquired enough money to put a deposit and first month's rent down on a fairly expensive flat in the West End of Glasgow. Do you know of any reason why she would want to get at you?" Peter looked genuinely frightened then, as if he had just learned that somebody had this grudge against him. Phil continued. "Do you know of any reason why Bruce Anders would have it in for you?" Peter's eyes shot up then, suddenly wide and acknowledging of the danger that he might be in. He had never thought of Bruce as a threat, simply because they had always scratched each other's backs. However, he had realised recently that Bruce wasn't a friend and that he would do anything to protect his own interests. Murder, though? Was he really capable of that? "I think you need to be straight with us, Mr Dow, because I believe that you are in very real danger." It was all it took for Peter to crack open and sing from the rooftops.

"Bruce paid me to get some permits put through sharp, without having to go through the usual application process. At the time, I thought of it as doing him a favour, and I wasn't really looking for remuneration." Phil looked sceptical, but he nodded anyway. "As time went on, he became more friendly towards me, and you have to understand that I don't make friends easily. So it was nice to have somebody who wanted me to go to his apartment in Alicante, and who would invite me to his lap dancing club for a free dance with some of the girls. He also hosted a few fund raisers for my campaign at his bar. Anyway, I found out recently that he had filmed me at the club." He looked at Phil and Donna and searched for judgement on their face. They both looked flatly at him, neither judgemental nor sympathetic. "I wanted those files destroyed. So I asked Dave to help me get rid of them. You have to believe I was as shocked as anybody when the club burned down. I did not ask him to do it."

"Mr King didn't start the fire, it wouldn't be possible, he was dead for hours before the fire was started." Peter looked shocked as he tried to grasp the confusing facts that lay out before him. His mind was bending, the alcohol corroding his thought process.

"Then, whoever killed him must have started it?"

"That would be the safest bet right now, Mr Dow." He looked suspiciously at Phil then, and waved his hands animatedly.

"I hope you don't think I had anything to do with it?"

"Mr Dow, if I thought you had anything to do with that fire; your backside would have been hauled to the station by now. What I do want to know though is what Mr Anders was blackmailing you with? I don't believe that his club was only a lap dancing club. In fact, I believe it to be a brothel. No lap dancing club in the city makes money from only operating in the daytime, and no lap dancing club would get the regular flow of successful men in an area that would draw attention to them attending. Were you paying the girls there for sex, Mr Dow?"

"No, I swear. I didn't pay. I didn't have to. No money has ever exchanged hands there. Bruce threw it in for free."

"Even if no money exchanged hands, Mr Dow, coercing sex for free is equally a crime." Peter's head hung down now, and Donna could see the shame glower from his forehead to his chin. She was surprised at Phil's lack of tact. After all, whilst Peter Dow was as corrupt a man as she had ever met, he had also been incredibly naïve to think that Bruce Anders would be somebody he could trust. For his sins, he had paid the highest cost as far as she could see. Donna spoke more gently then, trying to interject the sensitivity that she felt Phil was now lacking. She darted him a warning stare and turned back to Peter.

"What exactly did Mr Anders have over you, Mr Dow?" Peter sighed heavily, and sagged back into his chair. For a moment, life just escaped him and what they saw was an empty shell of a man who had lost everything and was ready to have the last breath drained from his body. There seemed nothing left for him to lose, and he must have conceded, because for the next twenty minutes he spoke about his various business dealings with Bruce. He also told them how Bruce had been blackmailing him with recordings he had kept of phone calls, CCTV videos of him in compromising positions with girls at the club and also the threat of harming those Peter cared about the most. As Peter unloaded enough information for Phil and Donna to obtain a warrant for Bruce's arrest, he seemed to become more desolate. As his face became more neutral, his lips twisted into a semi-smirk and he thought of the irony of his own corrupt behaviour. He finally felt liberated from Bruce's blackmail, of all the terrible things he had done, and of the mother that he had held on to the memory of for all of those years.

Phil and Donna entered the lift from the tenth floor a few minutes later. They had left Peter rubbing his head with his hands. In gaining information from him, they had helped him unleash all the little nagging demons that had held him captive for so long. Phil hadn't felt good about interrogating a man who was clearly in the throes of desperation, but without Peter's evidence, he wouldn't get that bastard Bruce. He knew now for certain that Bruce had been involved in the murders. What posed the biggest question though was the fire itself. It hadn't been Peter Dow. It certainly hadn't been David King. That only left Bruce Anders and Jennifer Dixon. They could have disposed of the body in a multitude of ways without having to burn down Bruce's biggest breadwinner. He was so hell bent on revenge against Kate Mulgrew that it didn't make any sense for him to have burned the place down.

As they left the building, they became aware of a gathering crowd. In the North East curve of the building, a woman was pointing up towards the tenth floor. As Donna and Phil's eyes followed the direction of her hand, they saw Peter Dow unload himself from his veranda. His arms were outspread as he came shuttling down towards the woman. She moved back and within a few mere seconds, Peter Dow had hurtled towards the ground and splattered across the tarmac. Every bone in his body was crushed and the sheer thud that was heard would resound through the minds of the spectators for hours and days to come.

36.

When the police came crashing through her front door at eight a.m. Jennifer Dixon was barely awake. She had heard nothing prior to them forcing their way into her hall. Her body froze and her stomach surged, not with the tangled knot that she might have expected but with a ticking bomb that threatened to explode and obliterate her. If she had felt the urge to run, it would have been too late for they were entering her bedroom before she entirely realised what was happening.

"Miss Jennifer Dixon, I am arresting you for murder..." Phil Morris looked at her with such disgust that she could almost feel it wrangle and tighten around her throat. "You do not have to say anything, but it may harm your defence if you do not mention when questioned something which you later rely on in court. Anything you do say may be given in evidence." She scowled at him as her arms were pulled behind her body and placed tightly in handcuffs. "Search this place and don't leave until you've found it." As it were, Jennifer knew they would never find the knife handle because she had thrown it into the river further down the Clydeside, and it would have been carried off to sea days ago. She was quite certain they had nothing on her.

"For the purpose of the recording, can you state your full name?" She had spent five tiring hours in a holding cell awaiting interrogation. By now, she was tired and hungry, and as irate as she could possibly get. She wasn't in the mood for this smart mouthed detective or his mute sidekick.

"Jennifer Dixon." She folded her arms defiantly and flicked her hair back with one nudge.

"What do you do for a living?" She eyed her solicitor, a blonde woman with a strong Irish accent who went by the name of Jane O'Reilly, and then moved towards the table.

"I'm between jobs at the moment," she answered flippantly and snorted indignantly.

"So how do you fill your days then? Do you have hobbies? How do you keep alert?" Jennifer pursed her lips nonchalantly.

"I read." Phil Morris was already becoming exasperated. She had worn his patience thin before he had even begun to interview her after she attempted to assault one of the uniformed officers who had been booking her in.

"What do you read?" Donna watched as she unlocked her arms and fidgeted nervously.

"I like crime fiction and biographies." This seemed to amuse Phil who smirked at the irony. She could be the subject of her very own hybrid very soon.

"When did you last work?" She seemed surprised by the sudden shift in the questions, which was exactly what Phil had hoped for. The best way to catch somebody out in their lies was to throw them curve balls at such a speed that they would eventually lose focus. It was how he operated, and it had never let him down yet.

"Last year," she drew her cheeks in and they could almost see her tongue move within her mouth. Soon she would start to sweat. Being accused of murder did that to a person whether they were innocent or guilty.

"I'll ask again Miss Dixon. When you were you last in employment; legitimate or otherwise?" He saw Jane O'Reilly spring to life at her side as she moved to the defence of her client.

"I believe my client has already answered that question, Detective." Her face was resolved and uncompromising, her tone brisk and unimpressed.

"So you've not had a job for over a year?"

Jane swiftly interjected once again, "She has answered that question. Move on!"

"When did you first meet Bruce Anders, Miss Dixon?" Jennifer looked down briefly and Donna suspected that she was calculating the risk of her lies.

"Who?" she finally muttered. Jane O'Reilly fell back and allowed the younger woman to take the lead again.

"Miss Dixon, we're not playing games. We have witnesses that can testify that you know Bruce Anders." His tone was harsher now, less playful and veering on the side of intimidation. Jane raised an eyebrow which was a strong enough warning shot to Phil and Donna. His tone became softer then. "I've got two dead bodies to account for. I have a video that shows you committing one of the murders. I have more than one reason to believe you're linked to the other. You're not doing yourself any favours by being difficult." He paused in the hope that she would offer something; anything, to fill in the tiny pieces of the puzzle that they hadn't quite figured out. "Let us help you, Miss Dixon. Tell us why you did it? Did somebody coerce you to do it?" Jennifer glared at him.

"Did somebody pay you to do it?"

She turned her head away.

"Is that it Jennifer? You haven't worked in a year? I can only imagine how much a grand, two grand, or even three would mean to you when you haven't worked in a year," his voice lowered, losing reverberation in the small bare room. "Anybody would be tempted in your situation."

She snarled at him, her lip curling irately.

"I can only say it one way, Detective. I didn't kill anybody."

"I have the video footage, Miss Dixon." She smirked then. Cocky little bitch, he thought to himself.

"Then I must have a double."

"Is this how you really want to play it?" He held his mobile phone up and hit the play button. Jane and Jennifer's faces were almost aligned as they stared at the grainy video file.

"I'm not sure how you can tell that my client is person in this video, Detective. It's so far away that you can't even tell what's going on. If this is the best you can come up with, then I'm afraid you don't have a case." Jane felt satisfied that she would walk Jennifer Dixon out of that police station any moment, but she hadn't tangled with Phil before. He dropped his phone onto the table and threw open a brown cardboard folder. It contained various sets of notes that Jennifer and Jane could hardly read upside down, crime scene photos and various official documents. Phil reached in and pulled the close up of Jennifer that had been taken from the video and pushed it in her direction.

"Are you still insisting it isn't you?" Neither woman on the other side of the table spoke now. Jane looked suitably beaten whilst Jennifer retained her last modicum of defiance.

"Miss Dixon, do you have sex with men for money?" Jennifer snapped her eyelids up and glowered.

"No. I don't work. I told you that."

"You're quite correct. You did tell me that. However, we have had statements that confirm you did indeed accept payment for sex whilst under the employment of Bruce Anders." Phil fiddled with various papers in the folder as if he were searching for more documents that would incriminate her.

"From who?" Jennifer rested her elbows on the edge of the table and smirked. She felt confident that there were no witnesses. She knew all the tricks that the police would pull out to try to catch her out. She wasn't going to fall for it.

"Do you know Peter Dow?"

"No," she said, too quickly to be truly convincing.

"What about Kathryn Mulgrew?"

"Who? I don't know any of the people you are asking me about." She sighed petulantly and slumped back into her seat.

"Where were you on the seventh of November?" The conversation took another sharp turn, cruising down a different path, and she suddenly looked alarmed.

"At home," she offered, again too quickly.

"Do you want to stop and think about it, Miss Dixon? It was a couple of weeks ago, so your memory might not be entirely accurate?" It was Donna who filled the silence now, her voice soft and comforting.

"My client answered the question, Detective." Jane twitched her nose, seemingly going through the motions now since it had become obvious that Jennifer Dixon was the most blatantly guilty person she had been asked to represent this year.

"Okay, so you were at home. Alone?"

"Yes, alone, Detective. What can I say, I like my own company."

"What address?" She looked enraged, her forehead furrowing into a frown.

"What the fuck are you talking about, what address? The address that you bastards came bursting in to this morning. Look, I didn't kill anybody, and I just want to go back home." She became instantly animating then, throwing her arms up and thrusting her fist dramatically through the air.

"We spoke to your landlord an hour ago. He confirmed that you collected the keys on the ninth of November, so how would it be possible to have been there on the seventh when you hadn't even started to rent the place?" He paused again, awaiting comment. When she said nothing, remaining entirely mute, he continued. "Where were you on the eleventh of November between the hours of seven and nine?"

"At home." Her voice had lowered again, and she seemed to calm quite quickly. It wasn't lost on him that she had a volatile temper or the speed at which she seemed to lose and gain control.

"You see how we're having trouble with your alibi, Miss Dixon? During the first murder, you appear to have been alone in a flat that you hadn't even rented yet. Then you claim to have been alone in the same place during the second murder and, yet, we have a video of somebody who looks remarkably like you at the scene. I've also seen your flat, Miss Dixon. Aside from anything else, I'm wondering how a single unemployed twenty-five-year old can afford to live in a six hundred pound per month rental." She felt the room sway slightly then. She had to think fast, but her head was pounding and she couldn't correlate her thoughts with what he was asking her.

"I get unemployment benefit and housing assistance," she retorted meekly.

"Your landlord said you gave him a thousand pounds in cash. You must be a good saver?" Jennifer shrugged her shoulders and tried to re-ground herself.

"Miss Dixon. Did Bruce Anders give you money to kill Jessica Dow?"

"No?"

"Did he give you money to kill David King?"

"No?" She was quivering now, a bead of sweat appearing between a growing crease upon her forehead. She was starting to feel quite under pressure sensing that her continual denial was futile. It would be easy to plead guilty, but the consequences terrified her.

"Did you know Peter Dow?"

"I already told you. No!"

"You've never heard of him? Not in the papers? Not at HEELS?"

"I told you, I didn't work at HEELS!"

"I didn't ask you if you worked at HEELS? I asked you if you had ever sold sex for money, Miss Dixon. You made the connection between the two." She looked at Jane for support. Jane simply lifted her hands and drew breath.

"So, I'll ask again Miss Dixon. Did you know Peter Dow?" Jennifer didn't speak then. Her breathing became more labored as the rising panic threatened to bring her hurtling to the ground. The world spun then, the room shifting beneath her feet. She looked back at Phil who smiled triumphantly. "You know that he died very recently. Threw himself from the tenth floor of a building, Miss Dixon. Do you want to know why?" She shook her head and felt as if her lungs were filling with air that wouldn't escape. "He killed himself because somebody brutally murdered his mother. Did you know Jessica Dow was his mother? Did you know that David King worked for him, Miss Dixon?" She felt sick. "I think you knew all of these things." He saw a tear fall then. He wanted to applaud. She was human after all. She might only be crying to save her own sorry skin, but it proved that she wasn't a psychopath.

When Jennifer had composed herself, Phil continued to speak. "I think you knew all of these things, and I think Bruce Anders knew all of these things. I suggest, Miss Dixon, that Mr Anders hired you when he learned that Mr King would be stealing back the files and recordings that he held on Peter Dow. I think he offered you money to kill him."

"No!" She whimpered. It was as much of a defense as she could muster as she felt herself go limp.

"I think you stabbed him to death. I think you went back hours later and set fire to HEELS because you knew it was the best way of concealing your involvement. I think Mr Anders believed you when you insisted that you didn't burn down the club because it hadn't been part of the agreement. But I think you did it, and you're now willing to let somebody else take the blame."

"No!"

"You used the same weapon, Miss Dixon. We found Mr King's DNA on the knife that we removed from Mrs Dow's stomach. What did you do with the handle of the knife?" She shook her head, and he could see her become quite visibly distressed.

"I didn't set any fire," she whispered.

"Were you planning to kill Kathryn Mulgrew next? Or were you happy enough to frame her for the fire?"

"I did not set any fire, I told you." She screamed the words until they echoed off the walls. Then she jerked upright and slammed her fists onto the table until she sat absolutely rigid.

"How much did Mr Anders pay you, Miss Dixon?" Phil asked crankily. She looked down and bit at her lower lip.

"How much?" His tone was stern, and she felt the coldness wrap around her. She squirmed then, finally realizing that her persistence of innocence was fruitless.

"I didn't set any fire," she whispered, turning to Jane as a torrent of tears finally fell from inside her eyes. She was panting now, and the sound of her wheezing filled the room.

"Miss Dixon, I'm charging you with the murder of David King who you did murder, against common law, on the seventh of November 2015. I'm also charging you with arson and perverting the course of justice when you did, against common law, conceal the murder by setting fire to your place of employment. I'm charging you with the murder of Jessica Dow who you did murder, against common law, on the eleventh of November 2015. Do you have anything else to add, Miss Dixon?"

"I didn't set that fire." It was her last line of defense, and Donna looked curiously at her. She was going to prison for two murders. Why the hell was she so definitively defending herself against the accusation of starting the fire? Donna leaned over the table as she stood.

"Well, if you didn't start the fire, then who did?"

"It was Kate Mulgrew."

37.
The road lay ahead like a broken ribbon; worn and fractured. Potholes scarred the side of ledges and cracked into the overused tarmac. The black Mondeo sat on the opposite side of the street, falling between a multitude of stationery vehicles of varying style and colour. Dusk was beginning to land, the last of the fading sun breaking through dipping clouds.

Dressed in a pair of oversized tracksuit trousers and a blue parker that she had acquired from Phil's wardrobe, Kate walked with both hands tucked into her pocket, and saw the street transition from a manic parade to a skeletal procession in mere minutes. She had made the decision not to remain a prisoner in Phil's flat and had risked the small walk from there to the local cavalcade of shops. The walk had taken longer than expected because she discovered that the safety of his flat only made her more frightened to venture back into the real world. She saw cars slowdown in every direction and feared that any moment now she would be pulled into the back seat of a car. She saw hefty men lurk behind lampposts, incongruently staring, but failed to notice the little dogs at the end of leads that made their lingering a little less menacing.

She walked absent-mindedly up the centre aisles of the local superstore and threw items into her basket with little consideration for her limited budget. Phil had left her a little cash for some necessities which reduced her anxiety about buying food. She scolded herself for allowing a man to pay her way and recalled vowing never to allow herself to be indebted to anybody again. Yet, that hadn't quite worked out for her. She hadn't discovered her independence, or found her own way. Instead, she had just fallen from the shadow of her former life into the grey abyss of the one she now found herself in. As she neared the end of the aisle, she saw her disproportionate body in the reflection of a small oval mirror on a flimsy bracket that had been screwed to the ceiling. She stopped dead when she saw the black circles around her eyes in glaring Technicolor. It made for a jarring and uncomfortable vision and for the smallest moment she wished for the days where she didn't look like the demons had unleashed and sucked the last breath from her body.

Kate felt a chill tickle the back of her neck before skimming down her protruding bones and seizing flesh. She suddenly felt as if she were being watched. The heaving basket of groceries drooped from her stronger arm and she wanted to simply drop it and run for the door. Until now, she had felt safer in the store than she had on the street. However, she realised there was nothing stopping her assailant from coming into the store and attacking her. She moved to the counter, missing half the items from her mental list, and watched ruefully as the check-out assistant took her own sweet time ringing the items through. Kate wanted to run. She felt a scream trap between her gut and her ribs again. Just like it had in Phil's flat. Fear had become a constant companion, and she no longer felt complete without it.

The shop assistant finally threw a handful of filthy coins into Kate's shivering hand and did nothing to hide her contempt as Kate tried apologetically to fill the plastic bag she had virtually thrown at her. She had sighed as Kate shuffled to the door of the shop and then looked back into the store suspiciously. Had the assistant known how absolutely decrepit Kate felt, she might have behaved a little more civilly, but instead she wore her own ineptitude like a well-earned rite of passage. Kate, herself, might have been feistier in return if she had been aware of the girl's rudeness, or if she hadn't feared that a man walking down the aisle empty-handed was about to kill her.

The street had become more desolate and bleak when she stepped out of the shop and into the tumultuous November wind. Her left shoulder sagged from the weight of her shopping bag. What weighed even heavier though was the knowledge that she felt no safer hidden in the outer reaches of Glasgow than she did in its lonely centre. She felt the predatory eyes descend upon her and she couldn't be sure if she had been found or if she had simply spent so many weeks miring in her paranoia that reality was no longer a support beam for her.

Kate had fallen into a daydream when she heard the slow burr of a car sidle up alongside her. She saw the wet drab world come back into focus as she realised that the car moved at the same speed as her. As the panic bridled within her, she considered that this might be the moment where she finally came face to face with the person who had been following her. There was an urge within her to face them and finally get it over with. There was a different urge, fighting internally within her, to drop her bag and run as fast as she could. She walked a little faster until she could see the underpass that led back to Phil's place. It levered her anxiety slightly to know that she wasn't too far away, yet far enough that she hadn't completely escaped the clutches of whoever was following her. Finally, as she was moments away from running into the underpass, the car swept into the last vacant space on the street. She turned; her face twisted in fear and saw a woman in a dark blue Fiesta even up the car against the edge of the pavement. Kate felt ridiculous as she stood in the woman's eye line like a hare in a flame and endured her maddened leer.

Kate ran into the abandoned underpass and found herself surrounded by litter and rising sewage under the arch of dank bricks. Except for the light that illuminated either end of the tunnel, it was like crawling through a darkened cavern. She wanted to touch the curved walls. To feel the slime and squalor and know that it was as bad as things could get. It wasn't. It was only a drop of oil in a vat of boiling acid.

As Kate moved back into the strip of light, wrapping the polystyrene bag around the joint of her hand, she saw Phil's block come into sight. It had once been a derelict rock that had risen across the wood side scree into fields that spread into the skyline. Now, it was a built up face for the nearing villages and towns that remained separate to the wilderness of the city. Fear continued to hold Kate in an iron grip as she made the final dash to safety. There was no car now, but it might as well have rolled right over her, flattening her to the ground. She had been through so much in the past two weeks that it was difficult to know what was real and what wasn't. She fumbled in her pocket for the set of keys that Phil had given her.

"Hello Kate." She moved into the dim hall of the ground floor and heard the deep familiar voice of a male. She tightened her hand around a set of keys and lifted her head. She gasped loudly and froze in place. She couldn't run. She couldn't scream. She was just there. She listened for her own breath. She couldn't hear it. If she died of fright there on the spot, she wouldn't be at all surprised. Rage smoldered around the edge of his eyes and then flooded like fire water through his veins. He felt his chest tighten. She was smaller than he recalled. Thinner, even. After a long pause, he finally spoke again. "I've been looking everywhere for you."

38.

"She's lying," Phil insisted as he sat in the staff room with Donna. She hid behind the steam of her mug and sipped on the decaffeinated coffee. It was tepid and lacking taste, but it was the first coffee fix she had enjoyed in more than twelve hours. It was just after six p.m. and both of them were perturbed by Jennifer Dixon's insistence that she had not set fire to conceal the crime of murder.

"How can you be so sure? What is it about Kathryn Mulgrew that makes you so certain of her innocence?" Phil winced. He still hadn't told Donna that Kate was living at his flat. Unbeknownst to him, she had sensed that he was hiding something for days now. What was he hiding from her?

"Of course Dixon set the place on fire. What else makes sense? Does she really expect us to believe that she killed somebody and didn't try to conceal the body? Surely, you're not buying it Donna?"

"She's got nothing to lose by telling the truth. She knows we've got her, Phil. Why the hell deny the charge that's going to give her the least amount of jail time if she's guilty of that as well." He had to admit she had a point. Who else could have done it though?

"It couldn't have been Kathryn Mulgrew. She had an alibi. We checked it and checked it." He was frustrated now. He had gotten to know Kate so well and he was certain of her innocence, even without the alibi.

"She did threaten to burn the place down, though." Donna wondered why he was being so defensive of the girl. Couldn't he even consider that her alibi was just too convenient? Maybe her claims that she was being followed were all just smoke and mirrors. Could Stevie Wright have gotten his nights wrong? But how would Kate know that Stevie would get his nights wrong? Even Donna was struggling to find a scenario where Kate would be guilty. She had given them her alibi. It had been checked out. She was in the clear. What were they missing?

"According to Bruce Anders. He is the only person who seems to have heard her threaten to do it," he offered, limply defending her.

"I don't know what he'd be achieving by throwing the blame onto her, Phil. Jennifer Dixon hasn't named him. We still don't have any physical evidence connecting him to the murders. Dixon is so convinced that she didn't set the fire that there would be no reason to suspect that Anders did anything at all. Perhaps she killed David King and Jessica Dow, and perhaps, by sheer coincidence, Kate Mulgrew set fire to the place as she had promised. Maybe you should just accept that this girl isn't who you seem to think she is." The words pierced at him more than he might have expected and he suddenly realized he felt more for Kate Mulgrew than he should.

"What did forensics say about the accelerant that was used?" Donna took one last gulp and slammed the mug on the table.

"Kerosene or some kind of fuel I think," he muttered absently. "Or Petrol." His eyes widened.

"What?" Donna watched him rise from his seat and sensed the realization. "What?" she repeated.

"I know exactly who set that club on fire."

39.

"Bruce, what the hell do you want?" Kate was still frozen in place, but his words had splintered through her. "How did you find me?" He looked demonic in the shadows. She finally heard her own shallow gasps as the sound of breathing returned to her, but she still couldn't find the urge to turn and run. He laughed then. A vicious bellow of laughter that made her skin tingle like flesh against the ice. Hadn't she suffered enough? What more could he take from her?

"I know you burned down my club, you little bitch." Suddenly he reached out and tugged her head back so far that she thought he might snap her neck. She would happily die now to escape his grip and his fury. Her broken human heart continued to beat, gaining pace and threatening to burst out of her chest. He laughed again, this time his mouth so close to hers that she thought he would rape her. She had hidden behind so many people for so long that when it came to this moment, she suddenly realized there was nobody here to save her. Not Flo; not Phil. Only she could save herself, she realized. She felt the steel ridge of a key nip at the skin of her hand and suddenly knew what she had to do.

As Bruce Anders put his long masculine hand around Kate's throat and tightened it, she felt the shades of agony and fear crash within her. Knowing that she had to act to defend herself, Kate dropped her carrier bag onto the ground. The thud startled Bruce and as he looked down, she brought her other hand up towards his face. She forced the end of the key into his eye socket and plunged as forcefully as she could. He suddenly loosened his grip and bellowed like a scalded beast. He threw his hands towards his damaged eye and let out a high-pitched scream.

"I'm going to fucking kill you. You're dead." Holding the keys as if they were her life support, Kate turned and pounded up four flights of stairs until she reached the second floor. Her heart threatened to explode, her lungs felt as if they might crush inside her and her throat stung from the sudden exertion. She fumbled with the key in her hand now and tried to force it into the keyhole. She then heard him stomping up the stairs, still grunting from the pain, and muttering about killing her. She couldn't get the key in far enough to turn. She shook it violently and heard him continue to climb the stairs. As he came into sight, she could see his lacerated eye, as blood dripped from his chin. She managed to get the key to turn in the door. He quickened his pace. He was now twenty yards from her. She managed to throw open the door then and saw him run towards her. As she slammed it shut, he howled. "Open the door, you little bitch. Your policeman can't save you. I'm going to rip you in two." She spun the lock so that the door safely separated them both. "There's no way out, Kate. Open the door," his voice was flat and commanding now. She ran as fast as she could to the lounge, grabbed the phone and hit the redial button. As the invisible cage closed in on her, she surprised herself by remaining calm and pragmatic. She could hear him banging on the door as she moved back down the hallway.

"I'm calling the police, Bruce." The quiver in her voice belied the calm she felt within. There was no viable exit, but she felt safer in Phil's place than anywhere else in the world right now. She had managed to escape Bruce's clutches whilst delivering a killer blow and ensuring that she, herself, remained unscathed. Later, she would fall into a heap and cry. Right now, she wouldn't give him the satisfaction. She listened to the persistent ring at the other end of the phone. When Phil didn't answer, she then dialed 999 and waited for the initial invitation to request assistance. He banged once more before he began to pound the door down with a foot. Her voice rose as she leaned against the door to prevent him from breaking it open. As the lock began to break against the wooden beam around the door, Kate let out a shallow scream. She dropped the phone and forced all of her weight against the door. Finally, when she and the door could no longer hold him, she ran for the bathroom. It was the only room in the house with a lock. She heard the crash as he gave one final ferocious kick. She knew it was only a matter of time before he broke down the next door because that lock was too flimsy to offer any real barricade. Her last hope had been the police, but a door and an angry man stood between her and the phone. She hadn't realized, but she was now soaked from perspiration. She felt the bathroom door beat against her back. He no longer hollered, or howled, but calmly set upon breaking the final barrier between them. She conceded defeat and moved away from the door. Finally, as she rested her arm on the brim of the toilet bowl, she sobbed into her arm and watched the door being torn from its hinges. She didn't scream then. She simply watched him hunker down as black tears stained her weary face.

40.
As he parked his car in the usual place, Phil Morris pulled his mobile phone from his pocket. Two missed calls. One from Donna, the other from his house number. As he had been driving, he had become more convinced that he now knew who had set fire to HEELS. He had left his previous notepad on his desk at home and needed to collect that for reference. He sat outside his house and, just for a moment, soaked up the silence. The weeks had been filled with noise. There hadn't been a moment of silence for as far back as he could remember. Now, in the cold dusk, he savoured a rare empty minute.

As he continued to sit outside his house, he rubbed his dog-tired eyes. This case had been exhausting. How could so many people make such a bloody mess? He exhaled all the emotions that he gathered up over the past few weeks. One of the first things you learn on this job was not to form attachments or get emotionally involved. It was also one of the first things you forgot. Humanity got in the way.

Then, as the street lights sparked to life, Phil stepped out of his car and moved towards the Perspex door. It lay wide open, which surprised him, because Mr Beaton was a stickler for security. As he entered the ground floor, he instantly saw the assortment of groceries scattered across the ground. He also saw the tiniest splatter of blood across the walls and darted for the stairs. As he reached the second floor, he could see his own door hanging from the hinges. He ran towards the entrance, terrified that he was too late, and looked on in horror as Bruce Anders pressed his hands against the lifeless woman.

Bruce Anders had his hands around Kate Mulgrew's throat as he forced her against the wall. She felt her windpipe tighten as she gasped. She couldn't move. She was trapped between a brute and the wall and she wanted to scream. Whatever formed within her stayed locked within her constricting chest. From the corner of her eye, she felt relief to see Phil race into the hallway. He rained down a blow on Bruce's head, which gave him just enough pause for her to grab his arm and pull it away. She fell to her knees and tried to suck all the air from around her into her lungs. She could see Bruce's forehead connect with Phil's nose as the two men became embroiled in a violent struggle. They exchanged several punches, not one harder than the other, and Kate could see the blood across Phil's face. The fight carried on out into the stairwell as Kate finally managed to regain her footing. She ran towards the lounge and fumbled about at the foot of the sofa. Where the hell was it? She had stored it here for safe keeping.

The grunts of the two men still echoed down the hallway as Phil pounded his fist into Bruce's face. If it hadn't happened so quickly, and he hadn't acted without thinking, Phil might have really savoured this moment because he had longed to smack Bruce in the mouth since the moment he had met him. Now, he didn't have time to enjoy it. If he didn't act quickly, Bruce would gain the upper hand and there was no telling what the bulkier man might be capable of. Suddenly, Phil felt himself pushed against a railing. The banister leaned over the next flight of stairs and didn't seem like a sturdy option. He felt it cut against his back and he shook with pain. His arms stopped moving as he tried to grab for the railing and push himself away. Bruce thrust his hand into Phil's chest and pushed. Phil could see that one of his eyes had been gouged quite deeply so that he was now only seeing through the other one. Then, as he was about to take advantage of Bruce's injury, the bigger man suddenly stopped in shock. From behind, he saw Kate pull a knife from Bruce's spine. The scream that followed was like nothing he thought humanly possible. The knife clattered to the floor.

Donna Barclay finally found Phil's house. She had been trying to call him to tell him that she was on her way. She parked her car across the street and looked up towards his house. The lights were out, but she could see his car by the side of the pavement. She had finally caught on to who had set fire to HEELS about half an hour after he had raced off. After trying to call him, she had decided to come to his house and they could make the arrest together. If she was honest, she wasn't quite sure how she would handle it if she went herself, and she knew that she would be on sure footing if she was with Phil.

She walked up the path and into the building. She moved past the mess on the ground floor and onto the stairwell. As she climbed the stairs, she could hear muffled grunts and broken sobs. As she came to the first floor, it became clear to her that it was coming from outside Phil's flat. The first person she saw was Kate Mulgrew who looked battered and worn as she shivered on the top stair. A bloodied knife lay on the floor beside her. Further along the landing, Bruce Anders groaned in agony as blood glued his shirt to his skin. Phil Morris stepped back out from inside his door, his face a bloody mess, and spoke into the phone. He looked as shocked to see Donna as she was to see the sorry state his face was in.

"What the hell is going on?" Her voice was strained, but commanding. "What is she doing here?" Phil lowered the phone from his ear and realised he was rumbled. He hadn't thought of the consequences of having Kate here, or how it would look. Now, he would face Donna's wrath, and he could already hear her tell him how stupid he had been to get involved and how he had only brought her to his house because she was beautiful. She would call him a pig, lose respect for him for a few months, and then realise that he was just like every other man she had ever met. Their relationship would even back up then. It wasn't the first time he had put himself in a precarious situation for an attractive woman that he had met on the job. Donna leaned over Bruce Anders who was very much alive, but in an unfathomable amount of pain. She wanted to laugh, to tell him that he had gotten exactly what he deserved. Instead, she moved towards Kate Mulgrew and touched her arms gently. "Come on, Missy. Let's get you inside."

41.

Phil still felt battered when Donna pulled her car into the kerb. Bruce Anders had been taken to hospital and treated for minor injuries. His eye would probably be defective from now on, but the stab wound to his lower back had missed all the major arteries and transpired to be quite uncritical. Donna had been saddened to hear that. For the moment, Anders was safely locked in a cell awaiting interview and was no longer a risk to the public. For how long, she didn't have a clue. Jennifer Dixon was taking the entire blame for the murder's, and had not only failed to implicate Bruce, but had actually categorically insisted that he had nothing to do with it. She really must be in love with him. Phil's arms and chest stung, so he wasn't in the mood to gloat. Instead, he was here to make an arrest that he really didn't want to make. The downside to the whole sorry affair was that the innocent had been punished much more than the truly guilty, but he had to uphold the law and adhere to every letter of it.

"We're here to see your husband, Mrs Walker." The woman looked startled as Phil and Donna held up their identity badges and pushed past her. Mr Walker was sitting at the dining table reading The Herald as they made their way into the kitchen.

"Why are you here?" Mrs Walker demanded as she scurried behind them. She seemed agitated today, much more than the previous time they had met her, and Phil felt sickened about having to take her husband away from her. He had no choice.

"Mr Walker, we're here to arrest you on suspicious of arson." Mr Walker dropped his newspaper and, as he stood, Phil noticed that the colour had completely drained from his face. Mr Walker looked at his wife sorrowfully, and she began to sob. Donna felt saddened.

"There was a fire. It was petrol. Can you smell it?" Mrs Walker said vacantly.

"Would you shut up about the damn petrol, Elena," he suddenly barked angrily. Mrs Walker jumped slightly, her lip trembling, and Phil thought she might burst into tears at any moment.

"Why did you do it, Mr Walker?" Bill Walker composed himself then, proudly pulling back his shoulders and walking round the table. He clasped his hands behind his back and spoke matter-of-factly.

"How did you know?" There was no denial. Just an obvious acceptance that the police now knew he was the guilty party.

"The smell of bleach initially triggered it, Mr Walker. Most people's houses don't reek to high heaven of bleach. Then, Mrs Walker repeatedly spoke about the smell of petrol. I thought it was because the fire had taken place next door, but it seemed so vivid to her that it nagged at me since." Donna and Phil exchanged a worried glance.

"I was sick to death of watching the depravity of that place and being able to do nothing about it. We spoke to the council. We called the police. We even rallied all the neighbours together and confronted that pig Bruce Anders. He laughed in our face. Then I heard that girl threaten to kill him and burn the place to the ground." Phil nodded knowingly.

"Tell us what happened on the seventh of November." Mr Walker walked towards his wife and put his arm on her shoulder. She looked less confused now, as if she had known all along and had been covering for him. Was it possible that she had?

"I had taken the dog out late that night. The last girl had just left. I saw somebody pick her up in a car. As I walked past the club, I saw that the door wasn't closed properly. I called in to see if anybody else was still there. At first, I told myself I was just being neighbourly." He looked as if he were being called back into that night and re-living it. Staring past Phil and Donna, he continued. "Nobody replied. Then, I thought about that Bruce Anders smugly laughing in our face and all of the filth we had seen. I didn't really think it through. I could hear the girl, the pretty one, screaming on the front steps that she was going to burn it to the ground. I wished she had. I acted impulsively. I went to the summer house, where we keep our tools and such likes, and I found the drum of kerosene." The trauma of his actions finally appeared to mirror on his face. "The drum was heavy and was spilling all over the floor, even when I came into the house. By the time I got next door, it was all over my clothes. I poured it over their main reception and into the back until I had none left. I thought it would put them out of business." He voice cracked then, and his eyes watered. "I swear I did not know there was anybody in there." Remorse spread across his eyes as they shrunk and single tears dropped.

"Mr Walker. You weren't responsible for the death of the young man who died in there. He was already dead. What you did, though..." Phil blew a heavy sigh into the room. " What you did was dangerous and stupid, and could have killed somebody. You and your wife were the most endangered." Mr Walker looked at his wife who had now rested her head upon his breast. Phil wasn't sure if he had ever seen a man decrease in age by ten years before, but he was sure that was exactly what happened when Bill Walker found out that he hadn't been responsible for somebody's death. "Why did you set fire to your summer house?"

"I had to get rid of my clothes. My wife had already started to complain about the smell of petrol. I couldn't just throw them away. So I set fire to the clothes on the spot where I had spilled half of the kerosene. It seemed sensible just to burn the whole damn lot down." Bruce had suspected that Mrs Walker's rants about petrol hadn't simply been the rants of a woman with Alzheimer's disease. Now that had been confirmed. She had been every bit as lucid as they were in those moments. He seemed agitated now. "I just wanted that low life out of here. We had to sacrifice everything to afford this house. There was no way I was letting those bastards destroy the value." He spoke animatedly, his free arm flailing around him.

"We understand, but this wasn't the way to do it." Donna spoke gently and tucked her head under his eye line. He wiped away the tears, relieved that he hadn't killed anybody and that his secret was finally out in the open.

"Am I going to jail?" His body had sagged. He looked like a little boy who had been caught stealing money from his mother's purse.

"That's not for me to say, Mr Walker." Phil felt sickened that he couldn't offer hope to the old man. He saw Mrs Walker move her head across his chest, unknowing of what was going on around her. He hoped to god that the Procurator Fiscal would take pity on them, considering the nature of the club that Bruce Anders had been running, and the other circumstances that had come to light recently. He felt sad for Mr Walker, a man struggling with the illness of his wife who knew him less day by day. Moreover, he felt sad for Elena Walker herself who could no longer comprehend the enormity of what had taken place. He wondered what she might have been like before the ravages of illness had taken her away from herself and left her in the clutches of despondency.

"May I call my son and ask him to come and be with my wife? I can't leave her alone." Phil agreed and offered to make Mrs Walker some tea to calm her shaking hands. What would become of her if Mr Walker did go to prison? Would her son take her to live with him, or would she be shunted into an old person's home where she would have the last nugget of familiarity cruelly ripped away from her. As the hours unfolded, and Mr Walker finally gripped the scale of his recent act, Phil became more and more concerned for his state of mind. He hoped to god that Bruce Anders would give something away that would incriminate him in the two murders. He wasn't sure how that might help Mr Walker, but it might give the poor old guy a fighting chance. For now Phil was tasked with reading Mr Walker his rights and escorting him to the station where, at seventy years old, he would find himself at the mercy of the criminal justice system.

42.

"Shall I tell you what I think happened, Mr Anders?" The only words that Bruce had spoken in the last forty minutes, since the arrival of his lawyer, were "No comment." Donna Barclay had become visibly stressed, but Phil Morris' resolve was stronger than ever. "You hired Jennifer Dixon to kill David King when you learned that he was going to break in and steal documents that you were using to blackmail Peter Dow. You see, we know that Mr Dow would assist in pushing through certain permits that allowed you to operate businesses that weren't specifically legal." He paused and watched for any change in Anders' body language that might indicate recognition. There hadn't been a single flicker so far. He had remained stone cold rigid.

"I think Miss Dixon was paid by you to kill Mr King. Now, she's not a particularly sophisticated girl, so a couple of grand and a big enough knife should make it an easy task. But Mr Dow still wasn't playing ball, was he?" Another pause. "So, you hit him where it would really hurt. You had already helped him by finding his mother, using some of your less illustrious contacts, so you knew exactly where to find her. If you take away enough from a man, then he's only going to buckle and play ball. Or, at least, that's how you would think it would work." Bruce patted his hand mockingly against his mouth and let out a loud yawn.

"Do you have evidence to support any of this, Detective? My client's a busy man, and he's already told you why he went after Mrs Mulgrew when you arrested him." If Phil had heard the lawyer speak, he certainly didn't show or acknowledge it.

"Mr Anders, how much did you pay to have Jessica Dow killed." Bruce shrugged; seemingly unaware of how much trouble he might be in. Phil's irritation had shifted to contempt, but he knew he had to remain professional otherwise he'd lose his head. Their evidence on Bruce was already held up by a thread.

"Is it not true, Mr Anders, that you had her killed out of petty revenge because her son wouldn't play your games anymore. You no longer had leverage over his illegal activities, so you had to find a different way of towing the line with him. It's a callous man who can do that to an old woman who had already lost everything, don't you think?" There was a grain of acidity in Phil's tone now as he thought of poor old Flo's last moments. He felt relentless, unchecked, stomach churning rage. For the old woman whose character was now replaced in his mind with a grey cold stone on a slab. For her son, who had been deprived of a mother-son relationship for more than half his life, and whose beaten and broken body now lay closer to her than he had probably been in fifteen years. For the elderly man and his sick wife who had been driven to an act of madness by Bruce Anders selfish callous business interests. Mostly for the woman who he had now fallen completely in love with whom Bruce Anders had stalked relentlessly for more than three weeks.

"You're not here to judge my client, Detective, only to establish the facts. So establish them." Bruce Anders continued to ignore Phil's questions, to answer "no comment" and, most infuriatingly, to snicker at any suggestion of repentance or guilt. His lawyer did most of the talking, insisting that his client had no reason to kill either of the victims, or to pay anybody to do it. Toxicity spread through the entire room as they presented Bruce as the innocent victim of a slur campaign, of a corrupt police force, and of a woman with a vendetta who had baited him into almost battering her to death. There wasn't a word strong enough to describe the hurl of Phil's disgust. Although, he had yet to find real solidified evidence to pin on Bruce. For now, he realised, he was stuck with a marionette killer in Jennifer Dixon. She was certainly guilty, and deserved a weighty prison service, but she was certainly not alone. Bruce Anders would go to court over the next few days and he would plead guilty to a charge of breaking and entering as well as assault and battery. The note would probably not even be presented because they had found no evidence that Bruce had actually sent it and he didn't own a vehicle matching Kate's description. Which only meant that he had also paid somebody else to participate in his sick games. He would probably be hit with a fine that he would pay from illegal monies and then, without any doubt in Phil's mind, he would be going after Kate Mulgrew. What sickened Phil the most was that there wouldn't be a damn thing he could do about it.

43.

Blue finally broke through the tapered sky at approximately two p.m. on the thirtieth of November. The snow had taken a sabbatical and now rested upon the wisps of fluffy clouds. Kate had drifted in and out of a variance of relief and that agitated shudder for the moment she thought her life was finally coming to an end. After all the times she had thought about dying, when it finally came knocking, she had fought back more than she ever knew she could. Now, fear had surpassed, and it was a strange sensation not to feel afraid any longer. Bruce Anders had come for her. He had powered through every obstacle in his way, held her in the cup of his hand, and she had defeated him.

She sat on the bed now, running her fingers along the split of a marine coloured duvet. She hadn't ventured into Phil's bedroom before and it shocked her that it wasn't the shack that every other room in the house was. Phil emerged from the en-suite bathroom, and she saw the water split upon his skin like atoms in a vacuum. It was also the first time she had seen him without his clothes on. He tightened the grip of the towel around his waist and smiled sheepishly. She retorted silently with a feverish pout. It was a dual that shouldn't, and probably wouldn't, ever come to anything. Right now, they savoured a moment that lingered between them and thanked god the other had come into their lives when they both needed somebody.

"You know he'll be walking out of that police station a free man. Any minute now!" She smirked. Of course he would. Men like him always did. "We'll get him on assault and battery, breaking and entering, but that's about it. He's got a clean record so he'll probably get off with a hefty fine and a court order preventing him from coming near you..." he paused for a moment and looked at her. Was she still too fragile for the truth, he wondered? "But I don't think that'll stop him." He didn't even need to complete the sentence. Even when it hung between them, she knew exactly what he was about to say.

"What about the murders?" She looked perplexed, and he didn't blame her, because he believed in a law that seemed to fail the innocent far more than it jailed the guilty. His frustration etched across his face, and crept into his voice.

"We've got nothing on him. The slimy bastard is as clean as a whistle. They're buying the theory that he came after you because he believed you burned down his club. Jennifer Dixon, for some inexplicable reason, is refusing to drop him in it." He buried his face in his hands and barely concealed his anger. "Fuck! The stupid bitch is willing to do twenty years to cover his back."

"So, he gets off scot free."

"I wouldn't say that. I'm not going to stop until I've got him locked up." There was a grim determination across his face now.

"Where does that leave me now? I can't stay here forever." He turned to look at her and saw the worry crack across her face.

"No, I guess not. I think you should go home to Hugh and Harry." He awaited her reaction which didn't come immediately. He couldn't read the various expressions across her face.

"I can't go back there. That's madness." She huffed.

"Yes, you can. He'll never look for you there. You'll be called as a witness probably, but until then, you can hide out and get to know your family again. You can get to know them in the knowledge that you're not incapable of love, and that you're not a monster, and most importantly that you're not your mother." She heard those words and felt them burn within her stomach. She wasn't a monster. She wasn't her mother. Somebody else had said it and to some degree, it made her feel vindicated.

"How can I go back to him now? After all, I've done? I might not tell him what I've been doing, but he'll learn about it when the court case comes up. Could you love somebody who was a prostitute?" She looked defeated and burned out and she had barely been able to conceal the bruises to her face with the little make up he had acquired for her.

"I already do." He turned away from her then, and she saw his face in the mirror, engraved with pain and sacrifice. She wanted to hug him then, to throw her arms around him and make love to him right there and then. To feel him throb inside her and feel loved. She couldn't have known until that moment that he wanted it just as much. Knowing that it couldn't happen and that she must return to her old life left her with a sense of grief that she had only known once. Not for the absent father who she had often wondered about but never loved. Not for the mother who she had wished dead until that death brought upon her the knowledge that she actually didn't care. Not even for the husband who had been distanced by her behaviour but had continued to provide her with a life that she had been too ungrateful to accept. The grief she had felt had been for the loss of her son Harry, as she realised that he was the only other person who mattered to her. So, she stood up and left the room. Phil had no more answers for her. And she had no more right to ask for them.

44.
As she climbed over flattened shrubs, she could see the house in the distance. Even terraced onto four more houses, it looked as desolate and grey as she remembered. As she neared, the trepidation rose, and she longed to recall a time where it hadn't weighed her down. The windows were blocked in grey, concealing the interior from intrusive eyes that might want to peer into the lives of those who wanted not to be seen. Minutes passed as she approached and stared up the pathway, leaning over a black iron gate, glaring at the peeling skin of the tattered door. Tears formed, against will, and trickled down her cheek. She scolded herself because she couldn't remember a day in recent times where she hadn't cried. In the cocoon of her own life, she had swum in endless despair, drowning in the bubble of her own loneliness. However, on the mean streets of Glasgow, she had learned of the real loneliness and despair that a person would endure. It all seemed so trivial now.

The doorbell chimed, distorted and out of tune. It echoed through the house, bouncing off walls and disturbing the tranquillity. Silence restored itself a moment later, and she listened for a sign that somebody still lived here. It brought back the memory all those days where, between the screaming bellows of an unhappy child, she had only known silence and the ache of her own self-loathing thoughts. The sky remained dry, but clouds lowered and threatened to crack open wide. It only lowered her mood more. She wanted to feel good about this. She had spoken to Hugh for over an hour on the phone, and they had both made promises that she wasn't sure they were able to keep. Now, she was so debilitated by her own self-doubt that she wanted to turn and run. However, from inside, she heard the key twist in the door and a crack of light suddenly appeared, illuminating her gaunt and weary figure.

He saw her quiver in the dark, and quickly threw open the door. Her lip trembled as they finally came face to face. The light of the rising moon drew shadows over her sinking cheekbones. She looked hungry. She looked tired. She looked like somebody he barely knew, but he pulled her into the hallway anyway. He held her tightly in his arms, and she thought he might cry, which was more than she could muster.

"Thank god you're home," he said matter-of-factly, and led her into the lounge. Nothing had changed since she left. An eighteen square inch photo of a two year old Harry still adorned the feature wall, shrouding the pale lilac flowers that stemmed across fourteen sheets of embossed wallpaper. A corner sofa, vaguely similar in colour and design, cowered in the far corner and she was alarmed to discover that she could remember every crease and bobble it had acquired. The floor was a murky brown wood that had been robbed of its natural sheen through the first year of Harry's circling baby walker. It was a depressing realisation that Hugh had been so stagnant in her absence that their life together and apart was exactly the same shade.

"You want tea, you're freezing? You want a bath?" He fussed over her, and still she was unable to speak. He removed her jacket, now too oversized for her prodding bones. She thought about how she had looked a few weeks earlier, when Florence had taken her into her care, and she thanked god that Phil had offered her a lifeline between times. She was glad Hugh, for all her disdain for him, had not had to see her in that state. He had asked during their phone call where she had been, but had respected her refusal to tell him. She would never tell. Even through her indifference to him, he was still the only person in her life who had ever looked at her like she mattered. He still looked at her that way.

"Where's Harry?" she finally asked, wearily. His face changed, revealing a beaming smile that indicated he was delighted that she had asked.

"Up in bed, I'm afraid. I didn't want to tell him that you were coming home until I knew." What difference would it make, she wondered.

"He probably won't remember me," she muttered, looking around the lounge.

"Of course he'll remember you, Kate. He's five," he snapped, and then allowed the smile to creep across his face again.

"Six months is a long time when you're five." She sounded cold, like she didn't care that he might not remember her. Yet, Hugh wondered if her bristly tone might be a mask for how frightened of his rejection she was.

"I'll make tea," he finally offered again. "Do you want something to eat? Are you hungry?" She was hungry; starving even. Yet, she didn't have an appetite. "You can't have eaten very much sleeping under a bridge," he continued, and she simply nodded her head in acknowledgement.

"I'll make the tea, would you mind running me that bath?" Her tone had softened now. Truthfully, she just wanted to breathe. She felt overwhelmed. She tried to imagine how he must be feeling now. When she had walked out, he probably thought she would be back in a few days. Then days would turn into a month, and he'd be stricken by worry for her safety. Then anger might set in as a month become months. Why wasn't he angrier, she wondered? He kissed her on the cheek, gently intruding into her space, but not pushing her far enough to feel like a trapped animal. Although, that was exactly how she felt. She wanted to see Harry; the little boy who she wasn't good enough to mother. She moved into the kitchen and filled the kettle. She heard Hugh pound up the stair, one step heavier than the last. Then, she could hear the water gush against the rusty copper pipes, eventually drowned out by the growing hiss of the boiling kettle. She sighed heavily, and willed away a growing feeling of discomfort. She thought about Hugh welcoming her home so willingly. His lack of anger still bothered her. Then she heard his words and felt startled and confused. 'You can't have eaten much...' he had said, and it echoed in her mind. She looked around the pale lime kitchen and allowed the realisation to burn and crush her.

"You can't have eaten much sleeping under a bridge."

45.

She heard the words over and over again. His voice streamed through her like a running audio track, and Kate felt herself fall against the counter. How the hell had he known where she was sleeping? She had told him nothing about where she had been or where she had worked. The sole focus of their telephone conversation had been to move forward and to find away where they could co-exist for the sake of Harry. He had delved into her psyche, but only because it had become so clear prior to her leaving that she had no self-worth. She could tell him nothing of her recent lifestyle because she felt an unbridled wave of shame. Yet, he knew! She caught herself against the fridge door and moved towards the lounge again. She could hear him sing upstairs, and his voice unsettled her now. *'... Sleeping under a bridge.'* She thought of everything she had endured over the past weeks and she wanted to climb into a dark hole and disappear again. He had been following her. Her gentle husband who she had so desperately wanted to escape and he had known where she was all along. He had been playing with her; teasing and taunting her at his will. In that moment, the betrayal stung more than a hundred blows from the likes of Bruce Anders. In all this time, she had thought of her own mistreatment of him. She had never considered that he might mistreat her, or hurt her in any way. Now, she felt drowsy in the knowledge that he was as capable, if not more so, of being a different person as she was.

Kate climbed the stairs warily, one hand on the wall, the other on the banister. As she peered onto the first floor, she could see him lean across the bath and stir bubbles into the water. There was a joviality that seemed false and out of sync with the revelation that he had been her stalker all along. He wasn't the man she had married. There was a darkness; something sinister that she hadn't seen. Had it been there all the time? Had she just not noticed? Was she entitled to feel aggrieved after all she had done and hidden from him? What if they were cut from the same cloth, hiding the same dark unfeeling nature, quashing their secret self's into a tiny hidey-hole that nobody else could see into? Except, now they could see each other as clearly as if they had always known

She stood by the toilet door, inches from his towering body, and watched him turn to look at her. A smile spread across his face. She longed to know what he was thinking. The trepidation fell through her, like sand through a sieve.

"You okay? Thought you were making the tea." She looked for an edge in his voice, something that revealed his true nature, but there was nothing different about the way he spoke. He stood up and reached for the door. She blinked with fright. "What's wrong? You look bothered," he lowered his voice now, barely more than a whisper. The air dripped with menace, lacing the scent of Eucalyptus with its ugly pungent aroma, and she felt it rest upon her throat.

"It was you," she finally said. He looked at her, a dead stare in his eyes. "It was you who has been following me, you psychotic bastard." Without warning, he reached for her throat, wrapped his hands around her hair and yanked her into the bathroom. Her throat still ached from when Bruce Anders had assaulted her. She let out a shallow yelp and heard the bathroom door slam shut. He pushed her hard against the wall and gritted his teeth so hard she could hear the crunch devour all the other sounds around them.

"You didn't think I was going to let you just walk out on me, did you?" She wrestled against him, but his grip was too strong. "You are mine, Kate, and I'll kill anybody who gets in our way. Whether they're paying or not." The realisation that he had probably been following her since day one sent a shudder down her spinal bone, and she pushed harder to get out of his tightening grip.

"Why? Why do you want me so badly? I don't love you. I'm barely capable of love, and certainly not for you." She hissed the words, the venom spilling from her spit.

"What about Harry?" he asked angrily. She wheezed, the grip of his hand creating a purple abrasion near the arch of her shoulder.

"Of course I love him. He's the reason I came back. He's the only one I am capable of love for," she was gasping her words out now, spluttering the words from deep in her chest. This must have angered him more because he suddenly grabbed the back of her neck and pushed her head straight into the bath water. She hadn't seen it coming, and he moved too quickly for her to react. She felt her nostrils fill with water as she forced her mouth closed. How long could she hold her breath? She thought of Harry, already living without his mother, and wondered if it would really matter if she died here in this bathroom. She remembered that night by the river, where she edged dangerously close to throwing herself in. Now, she could feel her chest ache as she tried to hold her breath. She thrashed her arms wildly in the water and felt her hands slap against the surface. She wanted to scream for help, but it came out as a mere garble inside a bubble of liquid. Then, suddenly he stopped, letting go of her just enough that she could pull herself from the water and slump onto the floor.

  She saw Harry stand in the doorway. He stared sombrely at her. Dripping wet, she leaned across and pulled him to her chest.

  "Mummy," he cried! She felt the love pound through her as she realised that he knew who she was. Her fears lessened. He hadn't forgotten about her. Maybe it was the one good thing that Hugh had done, talking about her, keeping her alive in her son's mind; *stalking her*. She saw him hover over them as she held Harry so tightly that she might crush his little bones.

  "Come on, Harry, back to bed," he ordered, with none of the usual parental gentleness that had filled her with envy. She held on. Harry had saved her and she wasn't letting go. Hugh leaned down and grabbed her arm, digging his nail into her hand. She let go petulantly and watched as he pushed Harry lightly into the hall. "Bed!" his voice was insistent now. So insistent that she saw the little boy cower with his fingers on his quaking lips. She could feel his little fear as he shook in her grip. Finally, she loosened her grip and watched him pull away. She stared into his broken little face and watched him disappear back into his bedroom. The door slammed shut with a dizzying thud. Before he could attack her again, she rose up and stood before him, her eyes burning with a rage that she had never felt before.

"Go on, you bastard, do your worst." He didn't need an invitation, but she gave him one anyway. He grabbed her face and pushed her back into the door. She felt her head thump against the breaking wood, and the pain of her skull taking the hit was almost intolerable. It was like no ache she had ever felt before, and she thought her head would be smashed into smithereens at any moment. As he rained his fist down upon her face and she pummelled to her knees, he smashed his fist again, but this time straight into her nose. She saw the blood spurt; a sickening gooey mess than spurted onto the floor. She didn't know how many times he had laid into her face, or how long it was going on for, but when she had finally taken enough she crawled across the bathroom floor. She rose to her knees, her entire body and arms trembling, and reached for the bathroom scales. Not contented with the brutal beating that he had already bestowed upon her, Hugh followed her into the centre of the bathroom. His knuckles were grazed from the sheer ferocity of the attack.

"Let me know when you've had enough," he jeered, no longer a man that she recognised. Through her swollen eye, she saw the rapture of his disgust and contempt for her. Maybe it hadn't existed before. Maybe the notion that she had slept with somebody for money and that there was no level she hadn't sunk to was enough for him to stop seeing her as a woman, let alone the woman he had once claimed to love. Maybe this was his involuntary reaction to the scorn he felt for her. Whatever the reason, she *had* had enough. So she picked up the bathroom scales and smashed him right in the centre of his face. He bellowed like an injured bear and fell back against the bath. She raced to her feet and grabbed the scales again. She saw the reflection of herself, her beaten face, and her determined expression stare back from the surface of the scales. He bellowed with rage as he flapped wildly into the water. He could feel the heat of the bath snatch at his skin and he tried to lift himself back out. He then tried to find his balance as the bathroom spun. His hands slid against the rim of the bath, and he felt terrified that one more blow might be enough for him to end up drowned at the bottom of the rising water. Focusing every ounce of consciousness he could find, he finally managed to climb out of the bath and slumped onto the floor. He turned his eye to look at her and saw the unyielding rage across her face. She struck him again. This time with more strength and more brutality, over and over again, until she was sure that he was unconscious. *Or dead*.

46.
Kate pushed open the bedroom door and saw Harry sobbing in the corner. She quickly raced over to him and stroked his face.

"It's okay, mummy's here baby, and everything's going to be alright." She wondered how she must look and suddenly recalled why there were no mirrors in the bathroom. She had destroyed them all. After Harry was born she couldn't tolerate seeing herself or her hideous reflection stare back. She pulled Harry to his wardrobe and rustled through a pile of tiny clothes. She pulled a t-shirt from the pile and quickly forced it over his head. She still felt numb from the utter shock of Hugh's attack. Whatever she thought she knew of her husband, none of it had been true, and she didn't even have the entitlement to feel aggrieved. All she knew was that he was dangerous, and that she had to get her and her son out of there right now. She pulled a pair of burgundy cords up to his waist and searched the wardrobe again for a jacket. She imagined that any minute Hugh would spurt to life, and she'd be unable to leave with her son. She frantically zipped his jacket and then ran to her own bedroom. Nothing had changed in there either. The curtains were closed, banning any natural light, and the bed spread was neatly pulled up to the cuff of the pillows. Her face still stung as she pulled the wet top over her shoulders and stepped out of her skirt. She found a pair of comfortable tracksuit bottoms and a knitted jersey. Then she pulled her winter coat from the same wardrobe that it had always hung in and wrapped herself inside it. It felt like a safety blanket then. She saw thirty pounds and some loose change on Hugh's side of the bed, so she stuffed that into her coat pocket and then hurtled back to Harry's room.

Harry still stood exactly where she had left him. He was pointing at something that was behind the bedroom door. Kate felt that little pit of resentment twist around a myriad of endless dread. Something must be lurking behind the door. Perhaps it was Hugh. Had he come to life when she was changing into the clothes she now wore? She stepped back to peer into the bathroom, but the door was closed just far enough that she couldn't see there either. She felt trapped, a tiger in a cage surrounded by hurtling bullets, and she wanted to collapse onto the floor and die. Instead, she grabbed the handle of the door and thrust it as hard as she could until she could almost hear the hinges crack. Then, she ran into the room and grabbed Harry. He was still pointing. She looked up, imaging that any moment now Hugh would step out from behind the door and grab her. Instead, she found herself facing a soft toy; Bertie. He had been calling for Bertie, she realised. She let out a huge sigh of relief and grabbed the toy and stuffed it into her pocket. She then grabbed Harry's hand and pulled him, a little too hard, into the hallway.

Harry trailed behind her as she burst out of her front door. She had been crippled by her own anxiety as she descended the stairs with him in tow and snuck through the front door. Now, as she left her husband battered and bleeding on the bathroom floor, she felt a sense of freedom surge through her. She had escaped. She didn't know how many more times she would escape the danger that she seemed to repeatedly put herself in, but for now, this freedom was enough.

Kate stood at the edge of the dual carriageway and watched the traffic race by so quickly that the colours blurred into a hodgepodge. She gripped Harry's hand tightly and waited for an opening. The middle of the road was a grass verge with barks rising into the skyline. On the other side, a church steeple rose from behind the branches. Could she go there for help?

"Mummy?" She looked down at Harry, who was pointing back in the direction of their house. She turned and saw Hugh race from their house and hobble quickly in her direction. Even in the distance, bloodshot and dishevelled, Kate could see the ferocity in his gait. She swept Harry up into her arms and prayed to God for a break in the traffic. He was gaining on her, and cars were spreading back into the distance for miles. She had no other option but to run and put some space between them. At first she thought she'd be quite safe with her son but, as she saw Hugh close the gap, she finally knew that even Harry couldn't stop him. She could still taste the soap from the bubbles tingle in the back of her throat, her chest still ached, and Harry was proving to be increasingly heavy in her arms. She felt his tears rest upon her cheeks. How the hell had it come to this? What had made Hugh snap? He had always seemed safe; reliable and boring even. Now, she didn't even know who he was.   Finally, the traffic broke. Quickly, adrenalin pumping up the arch of her back and grabbing hold of her, she ventured into the fifty yard break and prepared to lunge onto the middle island. Looking back, Hugh was trying and failing to dart between the endless stream of cars, which allowed her to break up the distance between them.

Then, like a gift from the heavens, she saw a bus pull into the bus stop. The traffic on that side of the road wasn't as heavy. Sweat poured from her forehead and touched the tears that Harry had left on her face. She navigated her way through the two lanes of traffic on the far side so that she could run towards the bus. She saw Hugh finally make his way into the traffic. He looked desperate now, his ferocity subsiding. She ran towards the single deck vehicle as the door snapped shut. The driver looked down and shifted into gear.

"Stop!" She waved her loose arm towards the bus, desperately hoping that he would look up and see her before he pulled away. The moon peered through the clouds and lit up speckles in murky puddles. As she looked over, Kate saw Hugh on the middle island and wanted to scream at him to leave her alone. She finally reached the door of the bus as it was about to pull away from the kerb. She banged on the door. "Please?" The driver looked up, irritably, and shook his head. "Please?" She was pleading. She could see Hugh through the glass on the other side of the bus, ready to make his final dart towards her. She thumped the door harder. The driver followed her distressed gaze and finally realised that this young woman must be in trouble. He quickly opened the door and allowed her and the little boy to enter. As quickly as he had opened it, he closed it again. She dropped Harry to his feet and allowed herself to breathe. It came in quick bursts at first, and then she let out a gasp. As the driver pulled the bus away, Kate saw Hugh lunge into the road in a final attempt to accost her. As he made it to the middle of the road, a car suddenly screeched to a halt. She watched in horror as Hugh flew onto the bonnet of the car and smashed into the windscreen. Everything seemed to slow down in Kate's mind then. She saw him collide with the glass front. Blood splattered across the broken glass as he was thrown from the bonnet and rolled along the tarmac. The car skidded to a sudden stop and spun on its back wheels. The bus halted and Kate moved up the aisle. She watched as Hugh lay perfectly still a mere ten inches from the wheels of the car that he had just collided with.

"Drive. Please Drive." The other passengers, who were slowly becoming aware of the unfolding situation, started to stand up from their seats. They could see the terror in the young woman's face and that she and her child, now disengaged from her, were in some kind of trouble. An older woman leaned forward and put her hand upon Kate's hand.

"Are you alright, dear?" Kate whimpered as she waited for Hugh to rise from the road. She could see the motorist now leaning over her husband and fumbling with his phone. Hugh wasn't moving. She knew it was wrong, but she felt relieved. Deep inside her, in that place that had protected her for so long, she hoped he died. She fell into a seat and reached out for Harry. At first, he stared at her, and then he ran towards her. She cried loudly then, years of pent up pain clashing with weeks of trauma, until she shook violently and cried into his soft hair. She saw a police car arrive. Then an ambulance. The night lit up with an array of flashing lights. As the other passengers fussed around her, and chaos rained down on them, Kate felt one minute merge into the next. Hugh was hoisted into the back of the ambulance and didn't stir. When she finally felt less afraid, she asked the driver to open the door so that she could alight. She went to Hugh then and saw that his face was so badly smashed that she barely recognised him. His forehead had become so swollen that it looked like it might explode. The rest of his face was masked by, what looked like, a gallon of blood. She thought that his face now mirrored who he really was. None of the kindness he had feigned, or that had wracked her in guilt, had really existed. He wasn't the solid, dependable salt of the earth man that she had married in the hope that he would make her feel like a human being. He was a cruel, manipulative beast who had revealed his true nature. Not to her alone, but to everybody who knew them. That alone would allow her to sleep a little tighter tonight.

47.

The wind was nothing more than a silent cry as Kate stepped out of the car and onto the murky blades of grass. Harry rushed around from the other side with Bertie in his hand. She looked down and saw his optimistic eyes and recognised the complete contrast between him and the towering stones that marked the final resting place of the hopeless. Six months had passed since that terrible night where truth had both imprisoned her and then, finally, set her free. Now, even the colder days were sunnier than she had ever remembered.

In one hand, she felt the tug of the gentlest pull. In the other, she felt the thorn of a single white rose nip her skin. Her life had always been exactly that; caught between the rose and its thorn. Now, she was here for closure. To finally lay the past behind her and move on with the child she never knew she could love so much. She had found joy in Harry in the past months, and she now knew what it felt like to be human, to love and be loved. She moved up the central verge and scanned the rows of names. Finally, she came to the one that she was looking for.

JESSICA FLORENCE DOW

She leaned in towards the stone and touched it. In her mind she saw the old woman's face, tethered by the aching years and relentless winters, and she felt true genuine sorrow. Flo had been more of a mother in the few short days they had spent together than her own had been in the seventeen years that she had tolerated her. She had never been to her mother's resting place. She had only dreamed that it must be a cruel dark place where souls went to the fires of hell. Even now, she couldn't find mercy for her mother. She could for Flo though, the straightest of souls in a twisted world. She quietly thanked Flo for her kindness and placed the flower on top of the stone. The wind blew then and carried the flower onto the grass. For a moment, she could hear the loom of Flo's voice, cackling under the surface of the lightest gale.

"Who is it, mummy?" Harry brought her hurtling back to reality, and she turned to look at his curious face. She rubbed her fingers across his fringe and smiled. He looked so much like Hugh that sometimes she had to flick the switch in her mind that brought her husband's face rushing to the forefront. Hugh was in hospital now, recovering from a broken back. There would be months of recuperation, and then a psychiatric unit. What she hadn't known was that Hugh had been diagnosed with a psychiatric disorder when he was fourteen years old but had managed to mask it with medication. When she had walked out on him, it had tipped him over the edge. The medication explained why he had seemed so unloving towards her. He hadn't been capable of passion because if he had, he would most likely have been psychotic. They had found the car that he had bought to stalk her with. It had been hidden away in a local lock-up which is why she hadn't seen it sitting outside the house. Neither he nor Bruce would be getting the sentence they deserved as far as she was concerned, but it would be enough for her to have the opportunity to move on with her life. She looked back at Phil Morris, who stood against the bonnet of his car. He waved at her and waited patiently for her to return to him. Then she looked at her son again.

"Just somebody who once showed me that it was okay to care." She looked back at Flo's stone and smiled again. "I hope wherever you are, you're having the time of your life."

A SAMPLE FROM IN THE WAKE OF DEATH

IN THE WAKE OF DEATH

BILLY MCLAUGHLIN

The flicker of blue lights jolted him awake as he became aware of the bloody taste upon his tongue. The sirens were a jarring howl that cut through the air sharper than a ten-inch blade.

Marc Adams crawled back to consciousness, his thudding heart providing a trance like soundtrack to the melody of the siren. His body shuddered and stiffened under the weight of the unbearable pain and, if he knew nothing else, he knew that it would hurt to move. How had he gotten here, he wondered? His eyes rolled back, blinking wildly in panic as he tried to digest the awful truth that had brought him to this moment.

The wail became a scream as the alarms continued to echo, now sharper, past the tunnel of his ear. Then came the pain; at first a dull ache, then tightening around his muscles and lungs and then across his skull. He wanted to roar because he had never felt pain like it. Then he could see the silhouette of moving shadows, but they drifted in and out of focus so often that he felt as if someone were in his head repeatedly flicking the switch on and off.

Marc heard the voices now. Could he move? Could he speak? What was his name? What followed was a confusing fracas of sound that only served to increase his anxiety. He tried to turn his head but the slightest movement sent an ache rippling through him. He could feel the warm grit beneath his finger tips and he thanked god, for it was the only thing that kept him in the here and now. Everything else swam in and out of focus, and all the voices sounded as one. He still hadn't been able to make enough sense to answer any of their questions. He was too transfixed in his need to answer all the questions in his own mind. Where the hell had he been? Was he driving? What time was it?

"Just try not to move, we'll get you to hospital as soon as we can." A steady voice called from above. He wanted to say 'Okay'. More than that, he wanted to scream 'Help me' and cry. The words and the tears didn't come, but the pain became so profound that he wanted to fall into a black hole and shut it out. To fade from the pain so that it was no longer his and he could no longer feel it. Figures came and went, sirens had been hushed and the blue lights that first brought Marc into the present flashed no more. His bones felt like they had been crushed beneath the feet of giants and his lungs felt as if someone had poured fire into them. Finally, he felt his body lift. Was he dying? The black sky and its shimmering spots came closer, and he was certain he could see the whole world turn.

Marc was placed onto a spinal board and two hard foam blocks were placed at either side of his head. He heard the sound of Velcro as somebody pulled it from one block to the other, fastening it gently. Then he was carried through a gathering crowd and hoisted into an ambulance. A tear slithered from the corner of his right eye, and he felt the blood swim into his saliva at the back of his mouth. For a brief second, as it tingled at his tonsils, he feared he might drown in it. He heard the thud of an ambulance door, and it echoed so loudly that he thought he was crashing through the windscreen of a car again.

"Just relax, Sir, we're taking you to the hospital, try not to move." The paramedic's voice was soothing, like one of those voices you hear on a relaxation track. Another thump. A memory returned to him then. It returned like an old forgotten movie and not the fresh vision that it should have been. Joel?

"Where's Joel?" he suddenly called out, his pain forgotten for a split second. The paramedic rested his hand upon Marc's shoulder and looked at him sympathetically. The ambulance began to move.

"Who's Joel?" The paramedic spoke with more authority now.

"My partner, he was driving." Marc could see Joel now, in the midst of his mind, laughing and fiddling with the music system as they fought over what song to play. The paramedic frowned because, when they arrived, Marc's broken body had been lying by the side of the road. There had been no vehicle anywhere that he could see.

"Wait. Are you telling me that somebody else was in the accident with you?" How could that be? Had the driver, this Joel that Marc kept referring to, simply driven off? He looked at Marc again and wondered what the hell he was supposed to do. "We didn't find anybody else. There was no car here," he finally replied, holding Marc's arm perfectly still. He could see the frustration in Marc's bloody face, but his main priority was keeping him firmly in place because he was afraid that if Marc moved a single inch, he would be facing a spinal injury.

"No, I'm telling you, you've got to help him. Joel was in the car with me."

Fifteen Weeks Later

I can't breathe! I'm suffocating! I don't know how I got here, but I'm trying to catch my breath. A moment ago, I'm sure I was resting on the shores of Loch Lomond, my skin brazing in the shallow wind beneath the scorching sun. Then, I closed my eyes. Just for a moment. Only to shake away the weary cobwebs of my recent fatigue. I wonder what time it is because I can't possibly know how long it's been since I lay on the grass embankment at the most Northern point of the sparkling lake. Why can't I catch my breath? Why does it keep halting at the rim of my lips?

I'm still confused. I lose time, and everything becomes blurred, which is why I might not remember being moving from my sun-trapped spot to this cold dark enclosure. I am still lying down, but I'm staring into nothing; an abyss of endless black, and I long to use my eyes again. The only sense I am left with is my hands. My hands ARE my eyes. I feel around myself and discover that I have very little space to move and I'm not sure that I want to anyway. I'm smacking my tongue against the roof of my mouth, trying to salivate. It's too dry, so I'm beginning to panic, because I still can't catch that elusive breath that might be all it takes to fill my lungs and quash this suffocating terror.

I can feel the rickety skelves of rotting wood as I rub my numbing fingers against the surface. Somebody help me, I want to scream, but I don't think anyone will hear me. Dirt has begun to fall through a crack in the surface of my living grave, and I realise that I must be underground. That is why I can't see. That is why I can smell the damp mildew of the rotting catacombs near the isolated lake. I remember them from my childhood; crawling in the damp until the hairy legs of beasts forced me screaming out into the daylight. There is no daylight now.

I'm gasping now and my body is dripping in perspiration. If I don't die of suffocation, I'll die of panic, I realise. I start to kick at the wood, but it only causes more dirt to fall on top of me and I'm becoming terrified that whatever lies on top will cave in and bring with it all the worms and beasts that burrow through the mud. This is not how I want to die. I start to call, and I know that I'm wasting the few short breaths that I might have left. It's a choice between dying one way or the other.

My body aches because I've been rigid with fear. I don't believe in God, but I pray that the whole encasement will not come crashing in on top of me.

My eyes throb because I've tried too many times to find something other than the darkness to focus my sight on.

My throat stings from the drought that my drying body has now endured.

As perspiration escapes from every pore, I run my tongue across my lips. It doesn't help my laboured breathing, but it does help a little with the cracks that are forming on the front layer of my lips. At least, for a short time. I hear a crack in the wood, but I still can't see anything. Then, in a split second, the surface collapses and a waterfall of brown water comes flooding into the tomb. With the last glimmer of hope now drowning, I pull back as much breath as I am able to harvest, and I let out a sharp piercing scream that I hope will drill through the rushing water and the soggy grains of dirt, but the scream simply spreads and dies inside the wooden tomb...